## *Krazy 4 U*

Abbie pushed the door open and stood frozen in the doorway, shocked into silence by what she saw.

Everywhere she looked, she smiled down on herself. The room was huge, obviously a converted attic, and Abbie filled every wall. Poster-size photographs of herself — more than fifty of them-dominated the room, with the smaller spaces filled in with eight — by ten-inch shots.

Pinned to the wall over a life-size print of herself, positioned to look as if she were wearing it, was one of her missing sweatshirts.

"This is insanity," she said finally.

**Look out for:**

**Also available in the Point Horror Unleashed series:**

*Point Horror*

# KRAZY 4 U

## A. BATES

■ SCHOLASTIC

Scholastic Children's Books,
Commonwealth House, 1-19 New Oxford Street,
London WC1A 1NU

New York ~Toronto ~ Sydney ~ Auckland

First published in the US by Scholastic Inc., 1996
First published in the UK by Scholastic Ltd, 1997

Copyright © Auline Bates, 1996

ISBN 0 590 19521 2

Printed by Cox & Wyman Ltd, Reading, Berks.

To those of my own best friends from school who have remained close — Phyllis Moberly, Barbara Kasbohm, Linda Lester, Jenie Leiper, Gloria Ulman and Tom Foote. You are proof that friendship is one of the most enduring forms of love.

And as always, Greg, thanks. It's a pleasure working with you.

# KRAZY 4 U

# Chapter 1

Abbie Grant stared at her friend, wondering exactly what to say. She swished her tea bag back and forth in her mug, finally just blurting out the question, "Do you ever have feelings?"

Across the kitchen, Taylor raised her eyebrows. "What are you asking? Am I numb? Of course I have feelings." She opened a package of chocolate chip cookies and dumped them in the cookie jar. "What kind of question is that?"

"I don't mean like that." Abbie stared into her cup. "I mean feelings like something's going to happen."

"Like a premonition?" Taylor shook back her shoulder-length blonde hair. "Nope. I don't believe in that kind of stuff."

Abbie, red-haired and green-eyed, gave her friend a long, thoughtful look. "I didn't used to, either," she admitted.

"Well, good. We agree on something." Taylor sat at the table, holding the cookie jar.

"No," Abbie told her. "I said I didn't used to believe. But it's happening to me. Ever since my parents left for Hawaii I've had this black cloud hanging over me. It's spooky, like . . ."

Taylor's laugh interrupted her. "It's just nerves," she said.

"No, I'm serious." Frowning, Abbie plucked the tea bag out of the mug with her spoon. "And I don't like it."

"You want some cookies or something?" Taylor offered.

"Too much sugar," Abbie said automatically. "Do you have any low-fat cheese and fruit?"

"Fruit has a lot of sugar in it," Taylor said, putting the cookie jar on the table.

"Fruit has fiber and vitamins. These cookies don't," said Abbie.

Taylor grinned broadly, and Abbie realized her friend had been teasing her — again. Taylor was a firm believer in junk food.

Laughing, Taylor scrambled out of her chair and opened the fridge. She grabbed cheese, apples from the crisper, and a carton of yogurt. "I wouldn't pay any attention to your black cloud," she said over her shoulder. She piled the food onto the counter, and got a plate. "Nothing bad ever happens to you, anyway. You lead a charmed life."

"I do not!"

"Do too." Taylor rummaged in a drawer for a knife. "You don't study and you get passing grades. If you decide on Monday that you're interested in a guy, by Friday you have a date with him. You . . . "

"That only happened once!" Abbie interrupted.

"So? It counts." Taylor sliced the cheese.

"I tell you, I'm worried. I'm having premonitions that something bad is going to happen, and instead of sympathy, you dredge up ancient history to try to prove I'm wrong."

Taylor brought the plate of fruit and cheese and plunked it on the table. "Here," she said. "Eat."

"Is that low-fat cheese?"

"It's·cheddar."

"Not low-fat."

"That's why I got out the yogurt. It's definitely low-fat."

Abbie sighed. "It's got added sugar."

"So you'll have to make a few choices," Taylor told her. "You can go hungry, you can just eat the fruit, or you can choose between fat and sugar." She grabbed the cookie jar, stacking cookies on a napkin. "I'm having chocolate, fat, and sugar, all in one."

Abbie put her elbow on the table, propped her chin in her hand, and stared at her friend.

"What?" Taylor asked, her mouth full of cookie. "You're staring at me."

"You did it again," Abbie said. "You have a talent for derailing conversations. I am trying to tell you something."

Taylor sighed. She fiddled with her teacup. "Premonitions aren't for real," she said finally. "And if they were for real, they would really scare me."

Exasperated, Abbie glared at Taylor. "That's what I've been trying to tell you! I *am* scared. I *am* jumpy. I don't know what to do about it."

"I can't figure you out," Taylor said abruptly. "It's like you want something to be wrong. Your parents are gone for three whole weeks. You have a gorgeous brother to share the freedom with, a charge card, a car to use, and a house full of food. That's as close to perfect as life gets, and you have to find something to complain about."

Abbie admitted defeat. "Okay. My life is perfect, at least for three weeks . . . although Brett can be worse than my dad sometimes.

You'd think he really was my big brother instead of a barely older stepbrother."

"There you go complaining again! If I had a hunk like Brett in my house, you would never hear me whine. Not ever!"

Abbie shook her head and opened her French book. I suppose he is good-looking, she thought. But he's been my brother for almost eight years. I can't look at him and see a hunk. I look at him and see the guy who taught me to swim and catch a baseball. I see the guy who treated me like one of the guys and not like a little princess. I see a brother.

She and Taylor drilled each other on French verbs, but Abbie's attention kept wandering. She felt edgy, as if someone were staring at her, wishing horrible things at her.

But no one was there except Taylor.

Slowly, Abbie closed her book, holding the place with her finger. Something bad was about to happen. She could feel it.

She focused on Taylor, trying to feel the air between them, to judge whether Taylor was miffed about something and not telling her, or just in a bad mood . . . or if somehow Taylor was really upset, really was the source of Abbie's uneasiness.

The longer she stared, the stronger the feelings got.

Maybe I should just leave, Abbie thought, reaching for her sweatshirt. I could grab my things and run.

She watched as Taylor picked up the knife she had used to slice apples.

Taylor jabbed the knife straight toward her, and Abbie froze.

# Chapter 2

The blade came straight at her.

And stopped.

"Do you want the last piece of apple, or can I have it?" asked Taylor, gesturing again with the knife.

When Abbie didn't answer, Taylor cut the last slice in half, then ate both halves. "What?" she asked. "You're staring at me. Are you okay?"

"Fine," Abbie said. "Just jumpy. I told you that already." I must be going crazy, she told herself. Taylor would never do anything bad to me. She's my best friend. She's been closer than a sister since junior high!

"You didn't eat anything," Taylor said, eyeing the empty plate. She sighed. "Which means I ate it all."

"You always eat everything," Abbie said.

"And you never gain an ounce. Anyway, I wasn't really hungry."

Taylor rinsed the plate and knife and put them in the dishwasher. "More tea?" she offered.

Abbie shook her head. "I've got to get going. I promised to cook tonight, and Brett is always starved when he gets home." She shoved her French book into her backpack. "He is not the most patient person when it comes to basics like food."

"He's got swim practice," Taylor said, sounding defensive. "When I went out for volleyball, I was starved when I got home, too. Sports takes a lot of calories."

"Right, okay, Brett is Mr. Perfect." Abbie popped her pen and notebook into her pack. "Whatever you say."

"I didn't say perfect."

"It's okay." Abbie slipped her arms into her sweatshirt-jacket. "I kind of like him, too." She fumbled with the zipper, finally getting it to mesh. "And I admit he's good-looking." She yanked the string on her backpack, closing it, and lowered the flap over the top. "I just didn't realize you were so enamored."

"I'm not enamored. I'm just looking, and he looks pretty good." Taylor handed Abbie her knit cap. "Okay, so he's a maybe."

Abbie paused in the act of slipping on her running shoes. "I've got one of those, too."

"One of what?" Taylor looked alarmed.

"Nothing catching." Abbie tied her laces. She looked at Taylor and smiled. "One of those maybes," she said.

"Who?"

"In computer lab," Abbie said.

"Who?" Taylor demanded.

Abbie shrugged. "He's just a maybe." She pushed the kitchen curtain back and looked outside. "Oh, no! Look at this! How can it be snowing?"

Taylor yanked the curtain farther open. "Yikes! It's barely October! Look at it come down! You didn't bring your mom's car, did you?"

Abbie made a face. "You know I like to jog. I believe in exercise. Besides, who expects snow this early in October? It was sixty degrees out there today!"

"Lots of exercise, no fat, no sugar," Taylor said. "Abbie, you're going to be the healthiest two-hundred-year-old lady on the planet!" She shrugged. "The *only* one, of course. You'll be lonely, but healthy."

"See you tomorrow," Abbie told her.

"Call me when you get home?"

"Sure." She's going to worry about me jogging a few blocks in the snow, Abbie thought, but the fact that I'm edgy, nervous, and being smothered in a black cloud . . . she didn't even want to hear about that.

Abbie headed out. The temperature was not that low, and the huge flakes melted as they hit the ground. But within two blocks the snow started sticking to the grass and sidewalks, and Abbie had to slow her pace.

Still, the early dusk had magic. The snow fell, isolating Abbie as she jogged. She could see a few feet in all directions, but beyond that, the thick flakes made a barrier of white.

This is all that exists, Abbie thought. Me, and the next few steps.

The streetlights flickered on in the growing dusk, making gleaming halos of snow beneath them. Abbie stopped suddenly, caught in a halo, almost overcome by the beauty of the lace curtain that fell in a circle between her and everything else.

"I love it!" she shouted, her voice muted by the snow. She laughed, thinking of her parents in the Hawaiian sunshine. "They don't know what they're missing," she whispered, turning in a full circle, her arms extended, snowflakes layering themselves on her sweatshirt-jacket.

The faint call of duty intruded on her dance,

and Abbie sobered, remembering that she had to cook dinner, had to be responsible and grown up, had to make sure Brett had a nutritious meal to eat when he got home from practice. A big salad? she thought hopefully.

She hurried on toward home.

He'd kill me if I tried to get away with just a salad! she thought, laughing.

She stepped off the curb, feeling almost lost in the quickly falling darkness, in the thick flakes that fell like a fog, shrouding her, limiting her vision. Every sound was muffled.

She quickened her pace.

A droning, rushing noise came at her, and Abbie whirled, peering through the shroud of snow. She couldn't tell what it was, or where it was until the vehicle leaped into her field of vision only a few feet away from her and nearing fast.

She felt like a deer frozen in someone's headlights, except there were no headlights, only a huge shape bearing down on her.

Screaming, uncertain which way to jump, certain only that she had to jump or die . . .

She jumped.

# Chapter 3

Abbie jumped sideways into the shrouded darkness and fell to the ground — hard. The flakes swirled madly around her in the wake of the passing car.

Adrenaline had poured through her as she'd stared at the car and leaped, and it coursed in her veins still, making her heart thud and her hands shake.

"You didn't even slow down!" she yelled, her voice trembling with relief as she suddenly realized she was alive.

*I could have died right here in the street!* she thought. *Would that lunatic have slowed down then, or just left me lying in the snow, bleeding . . . dying?*

Still shaking, Abbie got to her feet. Her knees could barely hold her, but she made herself look around, trudge to a streetlight, and get her bearings.

I'm only two blocks from home! she realized. I almost died just two blocks away from my house!

She started off slowly, shakily. Within a block the snow eased and Abbie could see well enough to look for cars at the last intersection she had to cross. Even though she could see the coast was clear, she still ran across the street . . . ran home.

The porch light was on, welcoming, which meant Brett was already home.

Abbie pushed open the front door. The trembling started up again the moment she was safely inside, safely home. Her stepbrother poked his head out from the kitchen.

"What happened to you?" Brett rushed to her, grabbed her by the arm, and propelled her into the kitchen. "You're bleeding. Sit down." He thrust her into a chair and grabbed paper towels.

Abbie started to lift a hand to her throbbing brow and stopped, startled at the blood that was dripping from her palm.

"You're a mess!" Brett handed her a damp paper towel. "Wrap your hand in that one," he ordered, dabbing at her forehead with another. "Look at you! What did you do?"

Abbie winced as he worked on her head, but obediently tended to her hand. Now that she could see the blood, her palm stung. So did her forehead. "Someone almost ran me down," she said, her voice shaky.

"In a car, you mean? On purpose?"

"I . . . it was snowing pretty hard. He didn't have his lights on. I didn't think . . . of course not on purpose! It was an accident. He just couldn't see me. Till it was almost too late!"

Brett looked at her, his face sober. "I think I should take you to the hospital."

Abbie felt her head, touched a lump that felt huge. "Ow!" she said. "It's tender, but I don't think it's all that bad . . . I walked home. I ran home, in fact. Seriously injured people do not run home."

"You should call the police," Brett said, eyeing her doubtfully. "And at least call the doctor. I've heard of people being in shock and not realizing how badly they were hurt. The folks left me in charge. I think you should call."

"They left us both in charge, and I don't think I need to call anybody!" What did I tell Taylor? Abbie thought. He's worse than my dad! "Brett, I'll be fine," she insisted. "It wouldn't do any good to call the police. I didn't see anything except this huge shape leaping at me out of the snow. I would feel really stupid reporting that. I couldn't even tell you what color it was."

"It just seems like we should DO something," Brett said, tossing the bloody paper towel in the trash. "Someone almost ran over my sister. I feel like I should take some kind of action."

"You can," Abbie told him. "Take my turn cooking dinner while I soak in the tub and check for hidden damage. Then make a huge pot of hot chocolate for you and some tea for me, and we'll sit and write a letter to the folks. And," she added sternly, "we won't mention this. There's no point in bothering them with something that's over and done with."

In the tub, Abbie had to admit she ached from head to foot. Which means I'll be all black and blue in a day or two, she thought.

She fingered the goose egg on her forehead, deciding that maybe a little creative work with the curling iron would hide it. The gash on her palm had bled a lot for a while, but it had stopped, and didn't look too bad. I must have hit something sharp with it, she thought. But I don't think it needs stitches. Just those butterfly bandages Mom has . . . they should hold the edges together.

In spite of hot tea, and Tylenol for the pain, Abbie slept poorly, her head and hand throbbing, the rest of her body warning her that her prediction of bruises would certainly come true.

In the morning, Tuesday, she surveyed herself in her vanity mirror and groaned. The swelling on her forehead had gone down in the night, but was still a lump, turning blue, streaked with red scrape marks.

No curling job in the world will disguise this, she decided, dropping the curling iron in disgust. Not even a complete haircut and re-style job would disguise this. I need a new face!

Abbie sighed. She ignored the throbbing in her hand as best she could and dabbed concealer and liquid foundation on the lump, gently patting on powder. She debated trying to disguise the whole mess with a dozen Band-Aids, but gave it up as hopeless.

In the kitchen, Brett examined her carefully, though at least he had the courtesy to be discreet about it. "You're walking slow," he said.

"I feel slow," Abbie told him, touched by the toast and orange juice he'd fixed for her. "But I'll be okay. Really I will."

"At least take the car?"

Abbie nodded. She usually jogged to and from school and only borrowed one of her parents' cars to go to work. Brett had his own car and drove everywhere, claiming he got enough exercise in sports. Today, Abbie would be more than happy to follow his example.

I'm only crazy to a certain point, she thought, assembling her lunch.

"I'd have done that for you," Brett said, looking apologetic. "Except you're so particular. I didn't know what you'd want."

"That's fine," Abbie assured him. "It was very nice of you to do breakfast. You don't have to baby me, Brett. I'm okay. Really."

"Well." Brett looked awkward, as if he didn't know what to say. "See you, then."

"Bye." Abbie knew Brett took the long route to school, usually picking up friends along the way. He'd never given her a ride, nor had she ever asked for one. They ran in their own crowds, rarely mixing except at home.

Abbie made herself a salad for lunch, sprinkled with gourmet salad vinegar. She packed extra carrot sticks, whole-grain no-fat crackers, low-fat cream cheese, and real, unsweetened apple juice. She added a handful of almonds and a home-bottled jar of decaf black tea.

Satisfied, she locked the house and drove her mother's Subaru to school.

It was a staid and sober car, responsive, square, very proper, and Abbie felt staid and proper by the time she was rummaging in her locker for the books she needed for her first two classes. But the near miss from the night before had also left her shaky — alternately frightened, relieved, and angry.

"You never did bother to call me."

Abbie jumped, startled at Taylor's sudden greeting. "Call you?" she asked, only belatedly remembering her promise.

"Why so jumpy?" Taylor asked, looking her over. "Wait a minute. Bruises? Bandages? Abbie, what happened to you?"

Briefly, Abbie filled Taylor in, playing down her terror and the rough night she'd just spent.

Taylor's eyes widened. "Abbie!" she said, grabbing her friend's arm. "How awful! You almost got killed!"

Abbie shook her head. "It was just one of those close calls. If you think about it, people have close calls all the time. It was no big deal, really. I shouldn't have been dancing in the street. I was dumb and lucky. That's all."

Taylor threw her arms around Abbie in an awkward hug. "I'm glad you're okay!"

"Me, too." Abbie felt her books slipping from her arms, dislodged by Taylor's enthusiastic hug. "Oops," she muttered, scrabbling with her arms, trying unsuccessfully to prevent the spill.

"Sorry." Taylor let go of Abbie, grinned at her, and knelt to rescue the fallen books. "What's that?" Taylor pointed.

Abbie looked. On the senior hall floor, a few inches from her sociology book, lay a sheet of notebook paper, pasted over with crude letters.

The floor was clean before, Abbie thought, reaching automatically for the paper. It had to come from one of my books.

Her hand trembling, throbbing, Abbie touched the piece of paper.

She read it, and her blood started rushing in her ears. Her vision faded, and she wondered if she were fainting.

"Taylor," she asked. "Are you there?"

"What is it?"

Abbie thrust the paper toward her friend. "Read it," she said.

# Chapter 4

In cut-out-of-magazine letters, like a primitive message, the words read, "B MOR KRFL U C IM KRAZY 4 U."

Taylor read the words aloud.

"Be more careful. You see, I'm crazy for you."

"Then it wasn't an accident," Abbie said, her forehead pounding. "Someone tried to run me over on purpose."

"No!" Taylor said. "Abbie, how could they? Who knew you were at my house? Who could have known when you were leaving, or which way you'd go home?"

You, Abbie thought, afraid to look at her friend. You were there when I left, and your parents' old car was there, too. It's a big car. And you know which way I go home.

No! she told herself. I'm being paranoid. It

wasn't Taylor. If Taylor wanted to hurt me, she's had thousands of opportunities over the last five years. No . . . it was someone else.

"Wait," Abbie said, shaking her head. "We're jumping to conclusions." She took a shuddering breath, stuffing her things into her backpack. "We're assuming last night's incident and this note are related."

Taylor nodded, her eyes wide. "Logical assumption, I'd say!"

"Maybe not," Abbie said, frowning thoughtfully. "It would be easy to slip a note inside my books during class or around school, but it's not so easy to open a locker. If the note was really connected to what happened last night, then someone would have had to put it in my book in my locker this morning. But that's impossible. Maybe it's been in my sociology book forever, and I just didn't notice it."

"I've heard there's some guy at school who breaks into lockers for money," Taylor said. "I mean, if you pay him to."

"Really?" Abbie slammed her locker door.

Taylor pushed away from the locker and headed toward the computer lab, Abbie beside her. "When two really bizarre things happen like that, right after each other, I suspect a relationship between them," Taylor said, looking at her friend. "So be careful on the streets."

Abbie pushed the computer lab door open. "So, I guess this disproves your theory that nothing bad ever happens to me."

Taylor rolled her eyes. "Can we go to lunch later since you have the car?"

Abbie nodded. "And my premonition was right."

Taylor plunked her books near her computer terminal. "Who's your maybe?" she asked, ignoring Abbie's last comment.

Abbie grinned, shrugging. "See if you can figure it out."

Abbie parked herself at the terminal next to Taylor, waving to others in the class, returning greetings. When class started, she tried to pay attention, but she felt restless. The note burned itself into her awareness, making her jumpy.

I still feel it, she thought. I still feel like someone's wishing horrid things at me. Isn't it enough that someone almost killed me yesterday? What else needs to happen? Why can't I shake this feeling?

She turned her head, scanning the classroom. These are my friends, she thought. People I've known forever. She looked speculatively at Clif Howard. *And my maybe.*

Clif was tall and slim, almost skinny. He had a thin sensitive face and a very high grade point average.

And he's nice, Abbie thought, remembering. She'd seen him stop in a rainstorm once and help someone change a tire.

Definitely a good guy, she decided, watching him work. She thought of all the other things she'd seen him do, simple things like being nice to people regardless of their popularity.

It's like he has a different focus, Abbie thought. We're all so busy wondering what other people think of us, worrying about whether we're doing the accepted thing . . . and Clif doesn't even seem to notice people are watching. I like that.

She realized she'd been staring at Clif, and turned industriously to the assignment. Her left hand hurt, making typing awkward, and she needed all her attention to avoid mistakes.

As class ended Abbie glanced again at Clif, thinking, *I gave Taylor a pretty big clue, staring at him like that.* She felt her face heat up, and looked away.

Taylor took her arm, drawing her into the hall. "A lot of things are suddenly clear to me," Taylor announced. "That was a most enlightening class! I'm glad you suggested I watch."

Abbie felt her face redden again. "So?" she asked. "What did you learn?"

"You mean besides the fact that I'm glad we have a program that checks my spelling for me?" Taylor was gesturing, whispering, being dramatic.

"Yeah, besides that." Abbie frowned at Taylor's antics.

"Somebody in that class has a big thing for you!"

Not Clif, Abbie thought. He didn't look at me at all. "Who?" she asked. "What kind of big thing?"

"Somebody spent the whole class focused entirely on you," Taylor said smugly. "And I couldn't tell if it was an 'I'm madly in love with you' kind of focus, or an 'I hate your guts' kind of focus."

"Quit being mysterious," Abbie demanded. "We've got to get to class. So just tell me, okay?"

"Somebody with dark eyes," Taylor said, drawing out her moment of drama. "Somebody who couldn't take those dark eyes off you the entire class. Someone who stared, and stared, and stared at you."

"Who?" Abbie asked, feeling exposed and alarmed. *How could I not have noticed?*

"I mean, if you've ever seen an obsessed

person, this is it," Taylor went on. "It was actually creepy. It got to the point where I wanted to get up and stand in between the two of you so he couldn't see you anymore."

Abbie actually felt chilled. Taylor's words were weaving around her like a trap. *Someone obsessed?* She shivered. "Who?" she whispered.

Taylor's eyes widened and she hissed, "Ssshh!" She glanced meaningfully over Abbie's shoulder.

Abbie swallowed hard and turned to look.

# Chapter 5

"Joey?" Abbie hissed at Taylor.

Taylor nodded.

"Joey Mowry?"

Taylor nodded again. "It's spooky," she said. "Just watch when you get the chance."

Abbie didn't know whether to laugh in relief or stalk away in disgust. "You can't be serious. Joey Mowry has had a crush on me for years, and you know it. I told you about him two years ago. You got me all shook up for nothing."

"It didn't look like nothing to me," Taylor snapped. "I'm sorry I mentioned it." She whirled and stalked off, her blonde hair circling like an arc as she spun.

Oops, Abbie thought. Now she's mad.

Abbie zipped into her seat just as the bell rang, trying to decide just how angry Taylor was.

I never know with her, Abbie thought, opening her book. She can be angry for days or just minutes. It's hard to tell ahead of time which one it will be. What kind of crazy friendship do we have, anyway?

And why is she making such a big deal out of Joey Mowry looking at me? Joey's been doing that for years. She knows that! Is she deliberately trying to scare me? She knows I've been feeling jumpy. She saw the note. She knows I'm already kind of scared, and then she tries to make me feel even worse!

By the time lunch break arrived, Abbie didn't know whether she should apologize to Taylor, or make Taylor apologize to her. She grabbed her lunch from her locker and hurried to the parking lot, where Taylor was leaning against the Subaru, talking with friends.

In typical Colorado fashion, all the snow from the day before had melted, and the air was almost balmy with blue, cloudless skies.

"Where are we going for lunch?" Taylor called.

Abbie unlocked the doors and climbed in. "Anywhere you like," she said, patting her lunch bag. "I have mine already, so we can go to any junk food shop that pleases you."

"That makes it easy," Taylor said. "The Burger Joint."

Abbie rolled her eyes, but she drove the

few blocks to the popular fast-food place. "Why don't I grab a table outside and you meet me there?" she suggested.

She had her food spread out by the time Taylor returned, loaded with burgers, fries, and a chocolate shake. "Mmm," Taylor said around a mouth full of fries. "Want one?"

Abbie cringed in horror. "Don't wave that in my face. Do you know what you're holding?"

"A french fry."

"Grease. Pure grease."

"It's good!" Taylor said, stuffing it into her mouth.

Abbie shuddered. "If I want a potato, I'll eat a potato," she said. "If I want grease, I'll crack open a jug of Crisco, thank you. I could drink it straight and get better quality grease than what you're eating."

"It wouldn't taste as good," Taylor said, calmly unwrapping a burger. She squeezed a ketchup packet, slathering the bun, making a big blob on the paper wrapper, too, for dipping fries in.

Abbie just shook her head. It was an old argument, and she knew they would never come to an agreement. At least she's not still mad at me, she thought. And I didn't have to apologize at all.

Taylor made a show of examining Abbie's lunch, then made a face. "You make a cute rabbit," she said.

"Rabbits don't drink tea," Abbie said, taking a swallow of hers.

"So what vitamins does tea have?" Taylor asked.

"This is just black tea," Abbie told her. "Not herbal."

"Decaf, I presume?"

"Of course."

"Why not just drink water?" Taylor asked. "Why drink lukewarm tea?"

"Black tea might help protect against lung cancer."

"You don't smoke," Taylor pointed out.

"Pollution," Abbie said. "It's unavoidable. It's everywhere."

Taylor shook her head. "You are a fanatic. Fanaticism is not a healthy state of mind. How can you live with what you're doing to your mind?"

"I am not a fanatic!" Abbie said. "I eat whatever I want. I happen to WANT to eat healthy foods."

"You are afraid of food," Taylor said smugly, popping another fry into her mouth. "You are afraid of life. You're afraid to eat, afraid to breathe, afraid to stop exercising. You look at life as if it were one giant disease trying its best to get you."

Abbie gave her friend an indignant look. "I'd like to point out what I am doing right now. Eating. Breathing."

"Oh, Abbie! You believe every article you read about the dangers of everything. You walk around petrified of food and air and pollution particles. If one article says eat spinach, you eat spinach. If the next one says put peanut butter on it, you do."

"I never put peanut butter on anything!"

Taylor grinned. "And that's exactly your problem, Abbie. If you can't find a study proving something is healthy for you, you don't eat it, read it, smell it, or do it. You never just give things a chance until they're proven harmful. You have to have proof in advance. You're a fanatic, and that's not healthy."

Abbie was caught short with no self-defense. Taylor isn't usually this good at arguing, she thought.

"Ha. Gotcha!" Taylor crowed.

"You've been working on this theory behind my back."

"You're right," Taylor admitted. "I've been thinking about it a lot. Because you just keep getting worse. You used to be reasonable.

Sometimes you would even indulge in a french fry or some ice cream. When's the last time you did that?"

Abbie just shrugged. "I haven't been in the mood."

"Right," Taylor said. "That's such a convenient answer, Abbie. Who has to be in the mood for ice cream?"

Abbie took a bite of salad and chewed deliberately. She ate some crackers and cream cheese. "I like this food," she said. "You are going way overboard suggesting I have a mental problem because I prefer healthy food."

"Yeah, just like I went way overboard suggesting Joey Mowry is totally obsessed with you because he couldn't take his eyes off you the whole class long, and because his eyes were practically burning out of his face."

Abbie wrapped up her lunch, furious. "Yes!" she snapped. "Just like that. He's been dreaming after me for years and you know it. I tell you that something bad's going to happen, and next thing you know someone almost flattens me with a car, and then I get a crazy note in my books. I need support and reassurance from my friends, Taylor, and instead, here you are, scaring me with this Joey thing."

"For your information, this was not a 'dreaming after you' kind of stare!" Taylor's voice was careful and precise. "Nobody would call it a dreaming look. This was pure, naked obsession. And believe me, after knowing you, I recognize obsession!"

Taylor hurled her remaining fries at the trash can, then clapped her hands over her mouth, her eyes growing wide. "Oops!" she muttered, her voice barely audible beneath her entwined fingers. "Speak of the devil!"

Abbie stared at her friend's startled face, but Taylor was looking beyond her, transfixed. Abbie whirled.

At first she was relieved. It was only Joey. But then she saw the look on Joey's face.

# Chapter 6

"Is she bothering you?" Joey asked, flicking a glance at Taylor. "Because I'll tell her to leave." His jaw was set, angry, and his eyes, dark and intense, darted between Taylor and Abbie.

"You'll do *what*?" Abbie demanded.

"I'll make her leave you alone." Joey glared at Taylor. "I saw her lose her temper. I saw her throwing things. People shouldn't act that way around you. You just say the word, and I'll make her leave."

All Abbie could think was, *He's nuts! This guy is nuts!*

Joey was still glaring at Taylor, and Abbie knew she had to come up with some kind of answer. "Joey," she said finally. "Taylor is my friend. Friends sometimes get angry and throw french fries. It's none of your business, okay?"

"As long as you're fine," Joey muttered, his face flaming. He looked sternly at Taylor, then turned and hurried off.

"You'd better watch out," Abbie told Taylor. "I have a protector. He doesn't let people throw fries at me." She zipped her sweatshirt-jacket, then tossed her lunch remains, still in the paper bag, into her car. She climbed in after it, shaking her head.

"I didn't throw them *at* you!" Taylor said, hopping into the passenger's seat.

"I know that." Abbie drove slowly, absently. "I've never seen him act like that," she said finally. "What was it all about?"

"I told you, but you wouldn't believe me. He may have just had a crush on you at one time, but the guy is obsessed with you now! He's had two years to work up to it."

"I apologize," Abbie said solemnly, pulling into the school parking lot. "I should have believed every word that came out of your mouth. You always tell the truth and never lie."

"Oh, shut up," Taylor told her. "I admit I have exaggerated at times in the past. How about a movie tonight? Do you have to work?"

Abbie shook her head. "Unless someone gets sick, I have the week off, till Friday." She grabbed her pack, locked the car. "A movie sounds like fun. What's playing?"

"I don't know. We'll check the paper. I'll drive if you like."

Abbie grinned. *If she drives, she picks me up, and she might have a chance to talk with Brett. Or at least look at him. If there's anything Taylor likes to do, it's talk to and look at guys!*

At home after school, Abbie checked the answering machine for messages, then made broiled, skinless chicken, steamed vegetables, and salad for dinner. Brett carried the dishes to the table.

"Thanks for cooking," he said, helping himself to an enormous amount of food.

Abbie filled her plate with salad, vegetables, and a couple of chunks of chicken. "We need a grain," she said.

Still chewing, Brett hopped up and grabbed a loaf of whole-grain bread. He handed it to Abbie.

"What? No comment?" she asked.

"My mouth's full," Brett pointed out.

"Good point."

"Otherwise I'd have thought of some smart remark about vitamins and fiber."

Abbie toyed with her vegetables, separating them into little piles. "Do you think I'm a fanatic?" she asked.

"Unquestionably."

"No, I mean really a fanatic," Abbie explained. "Like off the deep end."

Brett paused with his fork in midair. "You asked me a question, and I answered it. Rephrasing the question is not going to change my answer."

"Oh." Abbie used her fork to push the vegetable piles into one big lump again.

"You look like you're feeling better."

"I'm still sore," Abbie admitted. "I'll probably drive to school all this week. But at least the adrenaline is out of my system. Taylor and I are going to a movie tonight. Are you interested?"

Brett looked thoughtfully at Abbie, weighing the question. "Nah," he said.

Is he saying he doesn't want to spend time with me, Abbie wondered, or that he doesn't want to see a show, or that he suspects Taylor is interested and doesn't want to encourage her? It's so hard to communicate with people sometimes!

"It feels funny without the parents," Brett said abruptly. "There's no boss. The only rules we have are the ones the folks left. And it's really up to us whether we follow them or not. Who'll know?"

"As long as we don't trash the house or spend too much money," Abbie said, agreeing.

"So . . . if Mom gave me that stern look that means I really should stay home and study, I'd probably go with you to the movie." He carried his dishes to the sink. "Easy decision." He rinsed his plate, stuck it in the dishwasher. "It's harder when I have to figure out my own reasons for doing or not doing things."

He grinned. "I'm working it all out. Do you realize this is my first time without a mother, a teacher, or a coach evaluating every move? Mom got hyperinvolved in my life when Dad left."

Abbie thought about when her own mother died. Abbie had been eight years old, and very lost. Her father had alternated between being super attentive to Abbie, and being so depressed that he didn't seem to know or care whether she was in the house or not.

"I know," she told Brett. "When other people are around telling me what to do, I choose between obeying or not. But with no one to tell me, it seems like there are hundreds of ways to go." She shrugged. "Maybe that's what growing up really means. Looking at all the possible decisions and deciding for yourself which way to go."

Brett gave her an odd grin. "I'm working on it," he repeated.

There were thumps on the front door, but before Abbie could react, the door thudded open and Taylor entered, clad in one of Abbie's sweatshirts.

"How many more of them do you have?" Abbie demanded.

"What are you talking about?" Taylor cast a quick glance at Brett. "Hi," she said.

"Hi. What movie did you decide on?" Brett asked.

"My missing sweatshirts!" Abbie said. "I hope you're planning to leave that one here."

"Then I'd just have to borrrow another one to wear home. It's chilly out there!" Taylor pointed out. "The one the critics hated," she told Brett. "With worms crawling out of eyeballs and stuff."

"Yuck," Abbie said. She bit her lip, staring at her sweatshirt on Taylor's body.

"I've never seen a movie that got graded F before," Taylor said. "So it should be amusing. And since the reviews came out, all the seats are half-price. Can't beat that."

"I have lost three sweatshirts since school started," Abbie said firmly. "That's the first one that's showed up again, and I want it back."

"Fine." Taylor shrugged. "But not tonight. I'll freeze."

"So are you interested in the show?" Abbie asked Brett.

Brett pointed at the stack of books on the end of the couch. "Two tests tomorrow," he said. "I'm tempted by an F movie, I have to admit. But not by F's on my tests. Enjoy yourselves."

In the car, Abbie stared out the window as Taylor drove. Abbie watched the neighborhoods fly by, watched the homes change into business districts and the neon flash as downtown filled the windows.

Brett thinks I'm a fanatic, too, she thought. Not just Taylor. My own brother thinks I'm nuts. How can that be? How can I just go around living my life and thinking everything's normal, and suddenly find out other people think I'm nuts? Does everyone have this picture inside of who they think they are? Are other people's pictures of themselves wrong, too? Who decides what we are? Who defines us?

Abbie leaned her forehead into the heel of her uninjured hand and gently rubbed the side of her head without the lump. I could have died last night, she thought. Things change when that happens. Why can't Taylor understand that?

They turned into the theater parking lot and pulled into a space.

"Hey, ladies." A car pulled up next to them.

Abbie straightened at the unfamiliar voices. Guys. Taylor will enjoy this, she thought.

"Hi, guys," Taylor said. "You going to the show? I hear it's pretty bad."

Taylor was toying with her hair, smiling at the group of guys. Abbie had seen most of them at school, though she couldn't think of any names to go with the faces.

One of the guys grinned. "We're going to Mocha's for coffee. Care to join us?"

Abbie looked at Taylor, then back at the boys.

"Save us a seat," Taylor said.

The driver revved his engine, then the guys drove off.

"Let's go to the movie like we planned or just go home," Abbie said.

"The guys were nice, and I want a chance to get to know them," Taylor said. "I've got a life to live and I want it to include boys. These are boys."

"Half the world is male," Abbie pointed out.

"Half the world did not invite me to coffee,"

Taylor pointed out, starting the car. "These guys did." She eased the car back out onto the road.

"I'm tired," Abbie told Taylor. "Why don't you drop me at home, and then come back on your own?"

Taylor sighed. She pointed ahead and to the right. "There's coffee, lights, guys, and company," she said. She jerked her thumb over her shoulder. "That way, twenty minutes there and twenty minutes back, is your house. Would you please just come in and sit with us for a little while? It'll cheer you up. Then, if you're having a rotten time, I'll take you home."

"Next time I'm driving."

"Fine."

"Half an hour," Abbie said.

"Fine," said Taylor. "And, Abbie . . . thanks."

As they walked into Mocha's, a pickup truck squealed into the parking lot and slid into a space at the far side of the lot.

Abbie shook her head, her heart suddenly a lump in her chest. "It's Joey," she announced. "What is *with* him all of a sudden?"

The guys had saved them seats at their table, and the girls joined them. Taylor had coffee and a sundae. Abbie was vaguely aware of her laughter and animated conversation.

But Abbie sat, sipping decaf black tea and staring at the door, waiting for Joey to come in.

What is going on with him? she wondered. Why did he suddenly start following me around and staring at me?

Or has he been doing it for years and I only just now noticed because of what Taylor said?

She thought back over the last two years. She'd first become aware of Joey at the beginning of tenth grade when they'd been assigned a geography project together. Joey had turned red and stammered every time he looked at her. He was cute, and harmless.

Since then she'd caught him staring at her off and on, but all that happened was he would blush and look away when he realized he'd been caught.

That's a far cry from following me everywhere, Abbie thought.

Wait a minute! She sat upright so suddenly, she sloshed cooled tea on her lap and on the table. "Sorry!" she said, dabbing at her jeans with a napkin.

Taylor gave her a meaningful look, but Abbie was too preoccupied to try to figure out what it meant.

Joey was staring at me in computer lab,

Abbie thought. Taylor said she couldn't tell if it was love or hate. What if he doesn't have a crush on me anymore? What if he got tired of being ignored and hates me now? He's obviously following me, so he could have followed me to Taylor's and seen me leave. If he's been following me for long, he'd know which way I go home.

Was it Joey who tried to run me over in the road?

"I'll be right back!" she said, jumping up from the table. She rushed out into the parking lot.

"Abbie! What are you doing!" Taylor yelled after her.

Abbie ignored her, focused on one thing only . . . to confront her attacker head-on.

# Chapter 7

Abbie hadn't run five paces into the parking lot before she could see the truck was gone.

She stopped, turning in a circle, examining all the vehicles in the lot. None of them looked like the truck she'd seen pull in and park.

*Maybe that wasn't Joey after all?*

Confused, she examined the vehicles again, searching for one with a shadowy shape inside, watching her.

Nothing.

*Well, it was a great theory.*

"You could have just said you were ready to go."

Slowly Abbie turned toward Taylor's voice. "He's gone," Abbie said, nodding toward the corner.

"What were you going to do?" Taylor demanded. "Get a ride home with Joey? Are you crazy?" Taylor handed Abbie her purse. "You left this." She held out her sweatshirt-jacket. "And this."

"Let's just go home," Abbie said, shrugging into the jacket. The spilled tea made her jeans cling, icy on her thigh.

"I told them you'd been in an accident," Taylor said. "That you'd hurt your head and weren't quite yourself lately." She unlocked the car doors and gestured for Abbie to get in.

"Oh, great," Abbie said, climbing in. "Now those guys will think I'm a head case." She fastened her seat belt.

"An antisocial head case," Taylor told her, starting the engine. "Do you realize you didn't say two words the whole time in there, until you suddenly rushed off yelling? What is wrong with you?"

Abbie slumped in her seat. Her head and hand were throbbing again. "I told you I had a feeling something bad was going to happen," she muttered, switching on the heater.

They drove in silence for a while, but gradually Abbie's mood thawed and she told Taylor what she'd been thinking about Joey driving the car that had nearly run her down.

"Was it a pickup truck that almost hit you?" Taylor asked.

Abbie shut her eyes, remembering thick

halos of lighted snow, the sudden isolation as everything disappeared but fat snowflakes. She remembered the sudden noise and the shape emerging in a rush, directly at her.

"I don't know," she said finally. "I just remember it was big. So that could mean it was a truck."

"Color?"

Abbie shook her head in the dark. "I have a sense of color, but no specific recollection. It was a loud shape leaping out of whiteness. The only thing that really registered was danger, and I jumped. If I'd stopped to think what to do, or notice colors, I'd be dead right now."

"Joey drives a blue Toyota pickup," Taylor said. "And that pickup at Mocha's sure looked blue when it drove under the lights."

Brett was still up and studying when Abbie got home, and on impulse she stopped at the table where his books and papers and empty soft drink cans littered all the available space.

"Was the movie any good?" he asked.

"The whole evening was pretty much a waste," she told him, skipping mention of the group of guys. I don't need any fatherly lectures, she decided, finishing the tale with her doubts about Joey.

"Who is this character?" Brett asked.

Abbie shrugged. "Just some guy who used to have a crush on me. Only now it looks like more than that."

"Sounds like someone you should stay away from," Brett said.

"Like I have a choice," Abbie pointed out. "If someone's following you, Brett, you don't exactly have the option of staying out of his way."

She went to the kitchen and got two Advils, then returned and looked thoughtfully at her stepbrother as he turned back to his books. I wish I were as directed and dedicated as he is, she thought. He studies hard, gets good grades, plays on most of the sports teams, and is headed for college next year. He doesn't even let girlfriends sidetrack him.

"Well, good night, big brother," she said.

He looked up, faintly surprised, as if he'd already forgotten she was there. He gave her that odd grin of his again, and then went back to his books.

Somehow, his grin comforted her and made her smile. She was still smiling as she drifted off to sleep, still smiling until the first of the nightmares hit her.

It was the black cloud of premonition, only instead of a cloud in the sky, it was a mist that clung to her and she breathed it in like evil, choking on it. She felt it invade her pores and take root in her flesh.

It had eyes.

She sat up, shivering with fear, breathing rapidly. After a moment of remembered terror, she convinced herself that she was safe and awake. I will turn on the light, she told herself. And then everything will be normal again.

Thud. Thump, thump.

Her heart froze again, then pounded.

Someone . . . or some thing was just outside the house . . . outside her bedroom!

Thud. Thud. Thump.

Trying to get in?

Abbie was certain she could survive the nightmare and the thumping noises if only she could turn the light on. She would be okay if only she could see. There would be nothing to fear once there was light.

But she couldn't make her arm work to reach for the lamp.

The spell of the nightmare still held her rigid with fear, and the thumping sounded again.

Thud. Thud-thud.

*Like someone trying to kick a hole in the wall . . . or scrape their way through it.*

The nightmare is over, Abbie thought. And

now I'm awake. So why doesn't that noise stop?

I want it to stop!

Instead of stopping, the noise came again, nearer the window.

Thud, thump . . .

And then her window burst inward in a rain of glass.

# Chapter 8

The breaking glass broke Abbie's paralysis and she leaped from her bed, fumbling for the switch to her lamp.

With the light on, her room emerged from the darkness, ordinary, comforting, and sane . . . except for the shards of glass on the floor beneath her window and the hulking shape that leaned against her curtains from the outside.

Her eyes riveted on the curtains, Abbie felt for her shoes, slipped them on.

"Ab?" She heard running footsteps, saw the beam of a flashlight play against the curtains from outside. "Abbie? Are you in there? Are you all right? What's going on?"

Relief flooded through her at the safe, sane sound of Brett's voice. "I'm okay," she called. "What's that in my window?"

"A ladder. I heard noises and came out to check. Your window's broken!"

"I know." Abbie went to the window, glass crunching underfoot. She pulled the curtains back and looked out, shivering in the cool air.

"This looks like our ladder," Brett said. "Let me go check the shed." He loped off, returning in a minute with a hammer and a can of nails. "Door was wide open. Why don't you come and hold the flashlight and I'll nail something over your window."

Good old Brett, Abbie thought. Calm, take-charge Brett.

She grabbed her robe and another flashlight and joined Brett outside. He'd managed to locate a small stack of wood pieces and now he climbed the ladder and began holding them up one by one, checking their fit against the window.

"So what happened?" he asked soberly. "Who? Why?"

Abbie shook her head. "I have no idea. Why would someone bring our ladder over to my window? They couldn't get inside without breaking the glass . . . and breaking glass makes noise. It makes people come to see what's going on."

"Can you aim the light and hand me wood, too?"

Abbie nodded.

"I don't like it," Brett said. "I think I'll

get a lock for the shed tomorrow. Today, actually."

Joey, Abbie thought. It had to be. But why? What was the point?

"Whoever it was might not have meant to break the window," Brett said, pounding. "He might have heard me checking around and tried to get away too fast . . . might have clipped the window by accident as he moved the ladder."

That sounds like Joey, Abbie thought. He *is* kind of clumsy.

"At any rate," Brett said, "he's long gone, now. I heard a car start and drive off."

When the window was secured from the outside, Abbie went back in and cleaned up the glass, picking up the larger pieces and vacuuming the rest. She hung a thick quilt over the curtain rod to muffle the chilly night air, and spent the rest of the night with the lights on, sitting on her bed. Sometimes she dozed off, but she always jerked awake again, unable to really relax, unable to escape the black mist that fogged her dreams.

This is so incredible! she thought, staring as the digital clock blinked from 3:18 to 3:19. How dare somebody think it's okay to follow me around and spy on me? What goes on in someone's mind that he would think it was okay?

*And what if it wasn't Joey?*

Abbie jerked awake again just seconds before her alarm went off. She showered and got ready for school with the words echoing in her brain. *What if it wasn't Joey?*

The thought of Joey following and watching was bad enough, but he was someone she knew, someone she would always recognize and be able to watch out for.

*If this was the work of a stranger . . .*

She packed her lunch, wondering how soon the glass people would be able to fix her window. None of the shops would be open until at least eight o'clock, so she couldn't even call to make the appointment until after she was at school.

*If this was the work of a stranger . . .*

She looked thoughtfully at her bandaged hand, and felt her forehead.

# Chapter 9

"I do not believe in premonitions," Taylor repeated as they walked down the hallway at school.

"I had one and it came true," Abbie told her. "You have to believe now."

"What I believe is you were feeling a little scared because your parents are gone," Taylor said. "A house just seems different when the parents leave, and it made you jumpy. Maybe it was just coincidence that Joey picked last night to watch your house, or maybe he knew your folks are gone and figured he'd be less likely to get caught."

"What if it wasn't Joey?" Abbie asked.

Taylor stopped dead and turned to look at Abbie. The between-class crowd parted in waves around them. "You think it was someone else?"

"I don't know." Abbie bit her lip. "Logic says

it probably was Joey, but it could have been anyone. The same as that car coming out of nowhere could have been anyone. The only thing that limits who it could be is the note. It's not impossible for a complete stranger to put a note in my backpack without me noticing . . . but it's not likely."

"I've got to get to class," Taylor said abruptly. "See you at lunch?"

"Sure."

Abbie skipped her next class and phoned several glass dealers, but no one could get out to the house until Thursday afternoon at 1:00.

Not until tomorrow? Abbie thought, frowning. She made the appointment and tried to convince herself that wood was safer than window glass.

At least wood won't break, she thought.

At lunch she cornered Taylor. "I need to know for sure if it was Joey or someone else," Abbie said.

"Are you going to ask him?"

"No." Abbie shook her head. "I've been thinking about what you said . . . about somebody opening lockers if I pay him to? Who is it?"

"I don't know," Taylor said. "What are you planning to do?"

"Take a look in Joey's locker," Abbie said.

"He's not the only one who can play I Spy."

Taylor started to object, then she shrugged. She looked around the lunchroom. "Maybe those guys will know. I'll ask."

It took about ten minutes, but Taylor reappeared, towing a freshman by the hand. "George," she said.

"Ten bucks," George said. "And I never did it."

"What?" Abbie asked.

"If anyone asks, I never did it."

George used a thin, pliable strip of metal, which he simply inserted between the edge of the locker and the door, near the latch. He wiggled it around, then jerked it upward. The latch popped open. "Not that I do this often," he said smugly. "Mostly at the beginning of the year, when people forget their combinations." He sauntered off, Abbie's ten dollars in his pocket.

"What if someone sees you?" Taylor asked, looking around quickly, darting glances over her shoulder.

"I don't care," Abbie said. "I'm going on the offense, Taylor. I'm tired of having Joey watch me all the time, trying to learn everything about me. I think it's time to learn a little more about *him*. Let him figure out what to do about it."

Abbie shielded the locker with her body while Taylor kept up her nervous glancing, checking for Joey, or teachers, or Joey's friends. "Hurry up," she urged.

"Here goes nothing," Abbie said. She pulled on the locker door . . . and whistled. "Taylor, look at this!"

# Chapter 10

The entire inside of Joey's locker was papered with pictures of Abbie. Some she recognized from the yearbook, but others were shots she'd never seen before: obviously unposed, candid shots taken without her knowledge.

"That's clear back from tenth grade," Abbie said, pointing to a photo. "This is weird, Taylor! This is really spooky."

She patted the pockets of Joey's jacket.

"What are you doing? We've been here too long. Close it up and let's go."

Abbie laughed. "Look! His car keys!"

"You can't take those!"

"I just did," Abbie said. "Don't worry, I'll put them back." She pocketed the keys, grabbed a book from the shelf, and riffled the pages. "I don't believe this!" she said, holding the book out to Taylor.

"More pictures?"

"Taped in his books!" Abbie flipped through the pages of another, and then a third. "This is one obsessed nutcake if I ever saw one."

"What did I tell you?" Triumphant, Taylor took the books from Abbie, closed them, and slid them firmly back on the shelf. "Now let's get out of here."

Abbie used a piece of folded cardboard like George had shown her, jamming the latch so it wouldn't lock, then clanged the locker door shut. "This goes beyond flattery," she said. "This is sick."

"At least he had the good taste to choose you to be obsessed about," Taylor said, hauling Abbie by the arm, tugging her away from the locker.

"I don't feel honored," Abbie said. "I feel invaded. Let's go check the car."

But as they rounded the corner into the main hall, they nearly collided with Joey. He backed off, apologizing, but didn't retreat far.

"He missed you in the lunchroom," Taylor whispered. "I'll bet he's been looking everywhere for you."

"We can't do the car now, obviously," Abbie whispered back. "So let's go eat."

"You have to get the keys back before he misses them," Taylor hissed.

"Don't worry, I'll think of something."

What she thought of was a library pass during study hall. But instead of going to the library, she went to the parking lot.

She was still angry about last night's intrusion, the fright, the broken window, but as she reached the parking lot, she hesitated. Breaking into Joey's car seemed a lot worse than getting George to open his locker.

I'm not breaking in, she reasoned. I'm just unlocking the door and poking around, just like I did with his locker.

She looked around. Not all the students attended full time; people were driving in and out of the parking lot all day, some headed for classes at the community college, some to work-study assignments, some home.

In addition, buses came to pick up people for transportation to the career development school, or to ferry them back again.

Abbie felt exposed. There was no way to examine Joey's truck without being seen. And, she thought, I have to get the keys back into his locker before school ends.

I need to do this now, or not at all.

She thought of all the snapshots taped into his books, the photos — some enlarged to eight by ten's — papering his locker.

Okay, she told herself. I'm doing it now.

The first rule when doing something wrong is to act like you belong there. Do not sneak. Sneaking draws attention. Act like it's your own car.

She sighed. *Except I'm not even sure which truck belongs to Joey!* "A blue Toyota pickup," she muttered, scanning the lot.

It never seems this big when I'm looking for a space to park in, she thought, surveying the rows and rows of cars around her. She could see at least six blue pickups. She sighed again and trudged toward the nearest truck. *I'll try them all if I have to.*

The nearest blue truck had FORD across the rear gate, so Abbie walked on by.

The second was a Toyota, but it was occupied by a guy and a girl. The guy was staring down at his hands, gripping the steering wheel, while the girl, in a low but intense voice, was saying, " . . . rotten insensitive things I've ever seen you do, and you've done plenty, believe me. . . . "

Abbie hurried past, her ears burning as she tried to keep from eavesdropping any more than she had to.

"Hi, Abbie! Do you need a ride?"

Abbie recognized Clif's voice and turned around, startled to see him. She hadn't heard his car drive up.

Correction, she thought. His pickup truck. His blue pickup truck.

"Hi, Clif," she said. He talked to me! she thought, pleased.

"Do you need a ride somewhere?" He had his window down, his arm folded casually, resting on the window frame.

He was smiling, and Abbie, dazzled anew, smiled back. I don't know what it is, she thought. He's not incredibly handsome. He's not fabulous-looking. But that shy smile . . .

Suddenly aware she was staring like an idiot, she said, "Oh, well. I was just wandering around. Kind of." Oh, great! That made everything perfectly clear, she thought.

Clif nodded, but he looked slightly bewildered.

Abbie felt her cheeks heat up. Joey's keys burned in her pocket. I want to get in the truck and go somewhere with Clif, she admitted to herself. This is my first opportunity to be with him all alone.

"Where are you going?" she asked.

"Oh, actually I'm just coming back," Clif told her. "But I have an excuse, so I figured if you needed a ride, I'd just be a little later. No problem. Where would you like to go?"

Abbie fingered Joey's keys, torn. "Anywhere," she said. "Out of here."

"Hop in."

Abbie scurried around to the front of the truck. As she reached for the door handle, the little symbol she'd seen on the front grille registered. A sideways oval with two little ovals arranged inside to look almost like a bull with horns.

A Toyota symbol.

Uh-oh, she thought. What am I doing? What am I getting myself into? Can I get back out of it again? She paused, hand in midair.

Is this an incredibly stupid thing to do?

# Chapter 11

Clif leaned across the seat and looked at Abbie, his face concerned. "Is something wrong?"

"This is a blue Toyota," Abbie said.

"Which one don't you like?"

"What?"

"You don't like blue? Or you don't like Toyotas?"

"Neither," she said. "I mean . . . " She gave up trying to explain and just opened the door, climbing onto the seat. "Could we stop by the band door for a minute? I need to stop by my locker."

"Sure." Clif pulled the truck forward, idling outside the door to the band room, which happened to adjoin the senior hall.

Abbie hurried through the room, and on to Joey's locker. Now, don't look around, she reminded herself. Do not check whether anyone is watching you. Act like you belong.

She grabbed the handle and jerked upward.

The handle balked halfway, refusing to open. She jerked again, and again Joey's lock did not budge. Did Joey find the piece of cardboard and unjam it? she wondered. Did I put the jam in wrong?

"So what's happening?"

Abbie's heart felt like a fist had closed around it. She glanced over her shoulder and almost cried in relief when she realized the question was not directed at her. So far no one was paying any attention to her. But she also realized she could not stand around much longer, jerking Joey's locker handle.

She reached into her pocket, grasped the keys to Joey's car, and before she had time to get more nervous, stuffed the keys through the vent slots in the locker door. For a panicked second she thought they weren't going to fit through, but by twisting the key ring and shoving, she forced them in.

· They clanged to the floor inside.

Forgetting her own warnings about how to behave when doing something wrong, Abbie ran to her locker, dialed the numbers in a rush, and grabbed her pack, books for homework, and her purse.

She dashed for the band room. She had twelve minutes before the next class started.

In the empty band room she paused. Going to the parking lot during study hall for a sort-of-legitimate investigation was one thing. Cutting her last class to spend time with a guy was another thing entirely.

She reached for the door. It's only art appreciation, she thought. And I hate that class anyway.

Clif stopped for gas. He ran into the little store to pay for the gas and emerged with a paper grocery bag. He drove them toward the edge of town, to the low-rent business district.

"I work a couple of blocks from here," Abbie said, pointing. "At Positive Oats."

Clif laughed. "Positive Oats? What is that? A pet-food store?"

"Close." Abbie shrugged, self-conscious as usual when the subject came up. "Health foods."

"Health foods? Food isn't healthy all by itself?"

"You know, vitamins, whole grains, organic produce."

"Hmmm." Clif patted the grocery bag. "I may have made an error in judgment, then," he said.

Abbie looked in the bag. Laughing, she pulled out two jars of apple juice — from concentrate, sweetened — a small bag of Fritos and one of Ruffles potato chips, a twin-pack of Twinkies, and several candy bars.

"It's pretty bad," Abbie said, grinning at him. "But it was a nice thought."

"Keep looking," Clif told her. "I may have gotten something right." He turned into the crumbling parking lot of an abandoned building.

"Almonds! What made you buy almonds? I love them!"

Clif sighed in mock relief. "Not a total bust, then. Who knew?"

"That I was a nut about food?"

"That you work in a health food store, at any rate." Clif steered carefully around broken chunks of concrete and between gaping potholes.

"This is where we're going?" Abbie asked, looking out the window at the huge hulk of a building, once white, with smoke-blackened smudges at the broken windows, doors boarded up, and huge hunks of wall missing.

Clif edged the truck around the corner of the building. "It used to be a sugar mill," he said. "There was a fire . . . in the forties, I think, and some people couldn't get out. Burned to death. I guess they tried a few times to reopen it after that, but they just couldn't keep it going. It burned again in the sixties and they just left it."

As Clif parked the truck, Abbie could see the mill had been built in an L shape, with the long side facing the road, the short side of the L pointing across the grasslands toward the river, and the protected area inside the L holding the remains of what must have once been the grounds.

"I don't know what it is about this place," Clif said, turning off the ignition, grabbing the bag of groceries Abbie had repacked. "But I like it." He opened his door and stepped out, carrying the food. "Come on, I'm going to show you something."

All the warnings Abbie had ever heard streaked through her brain like alarm bells.

*Nobody knows where you are . . . nobody knows you're with Clif.*

Clif came around the front of the truck and opened Abbie's door, smiling at her, his eyes lit with secrets. "It's my own special place," he said.

*It could have been you at my window last night. You could have put the note in my book.*

"I found it a few years ago, and I've never seen anyone else near here. It's just my secret place."

*You could have tried to run me over.*

Clif held out his hand to help her down from the truck.

Abbie looked at the hand, a strong, thick hand . . . powerful. . . . She imagined it guiding the steering wheel, aiming straight at her, imagined the hand fumbling in the dark with the ladder, thumping it against the house, cracking it into her window.

Clif's smile slipped, and Abbie knew she couldn't just sit there. Time doesn't freeze, even if it felt like her body had.

She had to make herself smile at Clif, slide down from the seat . . . and run before he could grab her.

# Chapter 12

"What's the matter?" Clif asked.

Abbie swallowed. She looked into blue eyes, warm with worry.

"Are you all right?" he asked. "Do we need to go back to school?"

What possible reason could he have to wish me harm? Abbie thought. It can't be Clif.

She smiled brightly and took his hand. "I just get sidetracked sometimes," she said. "Let's go see this place."

Clif kept her hand, swinging it as they walked. "Actually," he said, "now that we're here, I feel a little silly. I mean, it's a kid's place, you know? I used to ride my bike here when I was nine or ten. You know how kids love private places."

Abbie liked the feel of his hand, liked walking with him. Her earlier doubts receded, almost evaporating as they crossed the weedy, overgrown grounds, which still showed signs of very old lawns and flower gardens.

Clif sat next to a long, wide row of wildly untrimmed shrubs that must have once marked the perimeter of the garden. With a grin, he moved a scraggly branch aside and crawled under the bush, beckoning to Abbie.

Wide-eyed, Abbie crawled after him and found herself in a tunnel. There were two rows of bushes that had grown together at their crowns, leaving an aisle beneath them, a long, shaded tunnel more than three feet high, tall enough to sit in and crawl through.

Enchanted, Abbie beamed at Clif. "I love it!" she said, her voice low. "It's magic!"

Clif smiled in relief. "Not too dumb, then?"

Abbie shook her head. "Not at all! How'd you find it? What made you look inside a hedge?"

"I can't exactly take the credit," Clif admitted, shrugging. "My dog ran in here once and disappeared. I followed him."

A lot of the leaves had fallen from the hedge; the rest were deep red-purple, dry and rustling, but Abbie could imagine what a shaded, leafy hideout this would make in spring and summer.

"So," Clif said. "Do you want to talk about it?"

"About what?" Abbie stretched out her legs, picked crinkly leaves off her jeans and dropped them on the ground. She turned her head and looked at Clif. He was close enough that she could smell his after-shave. The vaguely woodsy odor mingled with the damp smell of rotting leaves and the scent of fresh air, making a pleasant, mixed aroma.

"You're not all right," Clif said, watching her. "You're jumpy and nervous. You have all those bruises and that cut on your hand. Did someone hurt you?"

Abbie looked at her hand. The whole edge of her palm had been scraped and had scabbed, and the cut, though still bandaged, had begun knitting together. Her forehead had scabbed, too, but the lump was entirely gone.

"And a few minutes ago, in the truck," Clif went on, "you looked at me like I was an ax murderer. I mean, it may be none of my business, but I'm concerned about you, and if you need help, I'm here."

Abbie couldn't help the smile she flashed at him. His offer was so unexpected, but so . . . nice! "Thank you," she said.

"I mean it," Clif told her. "When a person you care about has been hurt, you want to do something."

The words echoed in Abbie's brain. Oh, she

thought, remembering. Brett had said something like that, too.

"So, anyway." Clif picked a leaf off her jeans and handed it to her, like a gift. "If there's something I can do, tell me, okay?"

Abbie tucked the leaf into her sweatshirt-jacket pocket. She shrugged, debating whether to blurt everything out or make light of it. The timing bothered her. He had barely spoken to her all year so far, and now, when strange things were happening . . .

"Why now?" she asked him. "Why are you suddenly concerned? Why not last week, or a month ago? This is practically the first time you've even spoken to me, and you offer me a ride and bring me here. Why?"

Clif looked down at his hands. He turned them over, examining both sides. "I've wanted to talk to you since school started. But I couldn't come up with anything to say. I'm . . . not all that good at this kind of thing. I mean, you never seemed particularly interested, and it's hard to just walk up cold and start a conversation. Today was the first time I had a reason and a chance at the same time. So I took the chance."

He looked up from his hands, his face expressionless. "I'm sorry it wasn't a good idea. Come on. I'll take you back."

Abbie shook her head. "Not a chance," she said. "You think you can promise me almonds and apple juice and then keep them all for yourself?"

Clif reached around in the paper bag, then grinned as he tossed her the bag of nuts. He handed her a jar of juice. "So, have you always been into health foods?"

Abbie shook her head. "My parents weren't," she told him. She opened the bag of nuts and shook a few into her palm. "I was never exposed to them growing up. I just . . . I got interested, so I started reading up on foods."

"What's so good about almonds?"

Abbie glanced up quickly, checking whether he was making fun. His face, no longer carefully without expression, showed interest, not ridicule. "I don't eat most nuts," Abbie admitted. "They're too high in fat. But almonds may help protect against cancer." She bit her lip. "Along with fresh fruits and vegetables, and whole grains. Almonds are a natural protein, too, and fiber."

"Like chewing a handful of wheat?"

"No." Abbie fidgeted, uncomfortable. She never knew how much people wanted to know when they asked about foods . . . except in the store, of course. Then they were really interested. Everyone else seemed to want to know just enough to make fun of her diet.

"I'm sorry," Clif said. "I always seem to say the wrong thing. Sometimes I think it's better just to not say anything at all. I do care about you. And I did want to find a way to tell you, to ask you out. I would have managed it, eventually. I was working up to it. Then you showed up all bruised and acting scared. Something bad had obviously happened.

"I wanted to try to help. I just didn't know what to say. So when I saw you in the parking lot, and you agreed to a ride, I brought you here. And managed to say all the wrong things. Can we start over?"

"My mother died of cancer when I was eight years old," Abbie said. "I needed to know why she got cancer, why she died, and no one could tell me. So I started reading everything I saw that mentioned the word cancer."

Abbie gritted her teeth, deliberately looking away from Clif, away from any sympathy she might find in his warm blue eyes. "I couldn't live her life over again, make it cancer-free. But I could do it with mine. I try to live an anti-cancer life, Clif. That's all it is. I know it's dumb in some ways, because she's already dead, and because even though I eat right, exercise, meditate, and take vitamins, no one knows if that's enough."

"I can see why you have to try, though," Clif said quietly.

"So that's why I'm prickly about the subject of diet," Abbie said, wondering how stupid it had all sounded to him. "And as for the bruises and what's wrong . . . it seems someone wants to hurt me."

"Who?" Clif demanded.

"Someone out there somewhere, and I have no idea who. Let's get back, Clif," she said.

Clif took her hand. Abbie resisted at first, stiff, wanting to keep him out, away. She'd never admitted to anyone the reason she was so careful about food, and the confession made her feel shy, as if she'd revealed too much.

But when he put his arms around her and hugged her, it felt okay again. It felt good.

"I'm sorry about your mom," he whispered. "It's so hard to lose someone you love."

Abbie squeezed her eyes against the quick sting of tears. The pain of losing someone gets easier to live with as time goes on, she thought. But it never goes completely away.

Clif pulled away and looked at her. He wiped the tears from her cheeks. "Now tell me more about the other thing," he said. "About someone trying to hurt you. What's going on?"

On the way back to school Abbie explained what had happened so far — her premonitions, the snowstorm and the car, the note in her book, and the broken window in the night. She left out the part about breaking into Joey's locker.

"So that's the story so far," she said as Clif turned into the parking lot entrance. "It's not so much, really, except the broken window, but it's got me spooked."

"I don't know what to think," Clif said. "It sounds pretty bad to me. Where did you park?"

"Um . . . " Abbie looked dumbly at the mostly empty parking lot. She pointed at an empty slot. "There, Clif! I parked right there! My car is gone!"

# Chapter 13

"Does anyone else have a key?" Clif asked.

"My parents keep a spare at home," she said. "But Brett has his own car, so he'd have no reason to take mine."

"Unless his broke down or something," Clif pointed out. "Is his car here?"

Abbie had been scanning the few remaining cars. "Nope. And it should be. He swims after school. His car is gone, too."

"Do you want a ride home? Or to the police station?"

"Let me just check at the office," Abbie said. "Maybe there's a message about it. There must be some explanation."

Clif followed as Abbie ran to the office, but there was no message for her. She raced to her locker, but there was no message there, either. She even opened the locker and checked each book.

"I guess . . . " She turned to Clif. "I guess if you wouldn't mind taking me home? I'll call the police from there."

"Sure."

"Let me run by the pool. Maybe Brett did something with both cars. Maybe he loaned them both out."

Abbie didn't believe it even as she suggested it, but she took off for the pool, only to find a note posted on the locked door. "Practice canceled. See you tomorrow."

"That explains why Brett's car is gone." Abbie leaned against the concrete-block wall, her head drooping. "I can't believe this! My stepmom's car!"

"Home, then?" Clif asked.

"I guess." Abbie pushed herself off the wall and plodded after Clif. It's too much, she thought. After everything else, a stolen car!

"So who took it?" Clif asked, snuggling his hand around hers. "And why?"

Abbie just shook her head. "I don't know. I wish I did."

Brett's car was parked in front of their house. Abbie dreaded having to admit to him the Subaru had been stolen. It was locked, she thought. It should have been safe!

She said good-bye to Clif. Then, reluctantly, she went inside to face Brett.

"So did you lock it?" Brett asked, pacing across the room and back, hands in his pockets. "My mom's going to kill us! That car was her baby! Isn't there any possibility you left it somewhere else, or loaned it to someone?"

"I think I would remember loaning the car!" Abbie snapped. "Leave me alone, Brett. I didn't do anything wrong. Somebody else did, and there's nothing I can do about it. I locked the car. I left it in the parking lot — where you leave your car every day, I might add. I'm as angry about this as you are, but just what do you expect me to do?"

She phoned the police and reported the car stolen, then called everyone she could think of to see if they knew anything. No one had seen anyone messing with the car. It was just gone. Taylor was sympathetic, but she flatly refused to discuss the theft as proof of Abbie's premonition.

Abbie hung up the phone. "Oh, no!" she wailed.

"What now?" Brett asked. "What else can go wrong?"

"The glass company!" Abbie said. "They're coming at one o'clock tomorrow. I was going to drive home to meet them." She sighed. "I guess I'll jog home at lunch and wait for them. No big deal."

Brett's anger faded visibly from his face, turning to concern. "I forgot about your window. I'm sorry. Here I am yelling like it's your fault." He turned away, jamming his hands into his pockets, glaring out the window.

After a minute he turned back around. "You can't sleep in your room," he said. "It'll be too cold, and besides, it just doesn't seem safe. Somebody broke your window."

"Yeah." Abbie tossed her hair back, bit her lip.

"I guess we have to assume whoever did it knew it was your window. That scares me, Ab. Please don't sleep in there."

Abbie felt suddenly chilled. "Did you get a lock for the shed?" she asked.

"What?"

"You said you'd buy a lock for the shed!"

"Oh. I did. I mean I bought the lock and the hasp to go with it, but I didn't install it yet. I'm sorry. If you want, I'll go do it right now."

"No!" Abbie told him. "I want you to put it on my door. On the outside."

Brett stared, then snapped his fingers. "Got it!" he said. "That way, if anyone does get into your room, they can't get into the rest of the house and find you."

Abbie slapped the arm of the couch. "That won't work!" she moaned.

"Why not? It's perfect."

"No. The hinges! The door hinges. They're inside my room. All he'd have to do is pop out those hinge pins and push the door open on the hinge side. What are we going to do?"

"The hardware store is still open," Brett said. "We can go look at what they've got. There must be some way of securing your door."

The realization hit Abbie that they needed to secure more than just her bedroom. "What's the use?" she asked, shaking her head.

"I'd like you safe!"

"Brett, there are other windows. We'd have to board up all of them and secure all the doors."

Brett looked at her, his eyes as grim as hers. "Spend the night with Taylor," he suggested.

Abbie rolled the idea around in her mind. *I might endanger Taylor if I stay there, but her parents are home. Wouldn't that be safer? Maybe, but is it right to chance endangering all of them? Who's doing this? Why? What do they want?*

"How about the basement?" Abbie asked.

She and Brett ran to check. "Hinges out

here in the hall," Abbie said. "That won't work. Garage, maybe?"

The garage was attached to the house, and the hinges on the door that opened to the garage were in the house. Abbie slumped against the door, shaking her head.

"Wait a minute!" Brett said, pointing at the bathroom door. "Those hinges are inside the bathroom. We can install the padlock inside and you'll be safe. There aren't any windows in there, either. It's perfect."

"What about you?"

"I don't seem to be the one in danger."

"If someone breaks in looking for me, and they find you instead, you think you won't be in any danger?"

Brett held up his hands. "Okay, I give. I'll go get another lock and put it on the other bathroom. I'll take the one upstairs, and you take this one. We'll have a jolly evening locked in the toilet. It'll be just like camping out."

"I'm sorry, Brett," Abbie said. "This may be my problem, but it looks like you've been dragged in whether you like it or not."

Brett shook his head. "It's not like you did it on purpose. I'll be okay . . . as long as the folks don't blame me."

"We're not going to tell them!" Abbie said.

"We're not going to be able to hide the fact that we installed padlocks on the bathroom doors."

Abbie grinned. Then she started giggling. At first Brett joined her and it was good to laugh. It broke the tension. But Abbie couldn't stop laughing until the gasps turned to tears. "It's so awful," she sobbed.

"I'll go to the hardware store," Brett said, turning away. He turned back and patted Abbie's shoulder awkwardly. "We'll be okay."

Sure we'll be okay, Abbie thought later. She was intensely aware of how frail their security really was.

Houses *seem* so secure, she thought. All that brick and walls and doors that lock. Windows that lock.

And all the time, all there is between me and anybody else is a thin pane of glass.

She put the cat in the garage and fed it, and made sure the garage door was securely closed. The cat door was tiny, too small to admit anything larger than an arm, and she made sure there was nothing within arm's reach of that door.

In the house, she checked each window to be sure it was locked, and the shades closed, even though she knew it was useless. She turned the heat down and made orange juice for the morning. She got Brett's coffee ready so all he had to do was turn the pot on, and set out her own tea.

I'm supposed to feel good now, she thought, lugging blankets and a pillow into the bathroom. I'm supposed to feel like I've taken care of everything, secured the house, and I can go to bed and sleep safe and sound.

And that's a laugh. I do not feel secure.

She grabbed clothes for the morning and put them in the bathroom, set up her bed on the floor, and slipped into her pajamas. She washed her face, brushed hair and teeth, and closed the padlock, making sure the key — and her purse, backpack, schoolbooks, and house and car keys — were safe in the bathroom with her.

Safe, she thought, snuggling down under the blankets. What a concept! Will I ever feel safe again?

Even though she left the light on, Abbie fell into a deep sleep, waking some time later to the sound of pounding on the bathroom door.

"You'd better get up and come see!" she heard someone yell.

# Chapter 14

Abbie knew it was Brett's voice, but she couldn't move. She didn't want to move. She didn't want to see any more ugliness. She just wanted to sleep, to have nice dreams and forget about whoever it was and whatever they were trying to do to her.

Finally she arched her back and looked at the clock on the bathroom wall. Six-thirty! She'd slept all night! "Okay," she croaked. "I'm coming."

She rolled over, untangling the blankets, and got to her feet. I survived the night, she thought. That's something.

Brett pounded again. "Are you okay in there? Abbie? Come on, answer."

"I'm okay."

"Put your shoes on, if you have them in there."

Mystified, Abbie slipped her shoes on and fumbled into her robe. She unlocked the padlock and opened the door.

Brett looked as if he'd run a marathon race. His face was sweating, his hair mussed, his eyes wild.

"What is it?" Abbie yelled.

Brett flapped an arm. "Come see."

Abbie followed him at a run, down the hall to her bedroom.

"I checked," Brett said. "Look."

Abbie opened the door and gasped. The boards that had been nailed over the window were gone and her room was a shambles — clothing strewn around, her dresser toppled, her makeup and perfume poured all over.

Abbie screamed, more in fury than fear.

"Nothing else in the house was touched," Brett said. "I thought . . ." He drew a deep breath. "I thought I heard something in the night, but I just . . . I fell back asleep. Oh, Abbie! I really let you down! I was going to keep watch, but I got so tired. I went to bed in the bathtub, but I promised myself I'd stay alert. And now look!"

"It's not your fault, Brett," Abbie said dully. "I'm glad you were asleep. You could have been hurt. I'd better go call the police."

I'll get whoever did this, Abbie fumed silently. He won't get away with this! "You go on to school," she told Brett. "I'll deal with the police and the glass company. It'll be okay."

"Okay?" Brett muttered. "This is okay?"

"Go. Go have breakfast. Pick up your friends and go to school." Abbie felt fragile, like the thin pane of glass that she relied upon to stand between her and intruders.

"I thought I was so smart," Brett said, wiping his forehead. "Putting on locks. It didn't help."

"It helped," Abbie said firmly. "We're both still alive. Thanks to you. Just let it go, Brett. You have to get your brain in gear and go be a good student. I'll deal with stuff here."

Brett finally went off to take his shower, eat, and gather things for school. He looked in on her before he left. "Abbie . . . thanks for dealing with this," he said.

Abbie grinned suddenly. "I slept very well last night," she said. "I didn't hear a thing. And I felt safe. You did good."

"Yeah, right." Brett clenched his jaw. His hands fumbled for a moment, then found their way into his pockets. "Do you think we should call the folks?"

Abbie sighed. She'd been trying to answer that question herself. "Let me talk to the cops. We'll see what they say. Oh, would you explain this to Taylor so she doesn't worry about why I'm not at school?"

"Sure. I'll try to find her."

"Thanks." Abbie understood what Brett didn't say, that college prep people ran in different circles from the regular people like Abbie and Taylor. College prep people studied in groups, took advanced classes, and didn't have time to run around looking for an average, ordinary person who didn't frequent the study lounges and advanced placement testing centers where Brett hung out.

Abbie had black, decaf tea for breakfast, along with whole-grain toast, and plain yogurt with wheat germ sprinkled on it. She wanted to clean the mess in her room, but she told herself over and over, don't disturb the crime scene. There might be fingerprints. There might be evidence.

When the phone rang, she jumped. "Hello?"

"Abbie, it's Clif. I'm hearing rumors your house was trashed. Is that true? Are you all right? Should I come over?"

Abbie relaxed, imagining Clif's smile, his warm blue eyes. She wanted nothing more than to feel his arms around her, hugging her, making her feel secure.

Nothing is secure! she reminded herself.

"Clif?" Through the window she could see a police cruiser pulling up in front of the house. "The police are here. I'm fine. I'll talk to you later, okay?"

She crashed the phone onto the wall and went to admit the police. The two officers, a man and a woman, seemed on edge, as if unsure whether Abbie's call had been a crank call or not. Or maybe wondering if the intruder were still inside. . . .

Abbie suddenly wondered the same thing herself. "I didn't think to look in the basement!" she said. "I checked the rest of the house. My room's that way. That's where the damage was done."

The officers checked the house, including the basement, garage, and yard, before they entered Abbie's room.

"Did you touch anything?" the woman asked.

Abbie shook her head. She explained about the broken window the night before, about her parents being gone, about spending the night in the bathroom.

"I think you probably should consider calling

your parents," the woman said, scribbling in a notebook. "Isn't there" — she flipped pages — "a stolen car from this address, too?"

Abbie nodded. "It was stolen from school, though."

"We can check for fingerprints," the man said. "But any fool knows to wear gloves these days. It sounds like someone isn't happy with you."

"Maybe it's someone who knows your parents are gone and thinks the house is just an easy target," said the woman.

Right, Abbie thought. They break into MY room and trash MY stuff and they're just looking for an easy target? They didn't take anything! "They didn't do anything to the rest of the house," Abbie pointed out.

"Something probably scared them off," the man said. "Or else they were specifically targeting you. This looks like typical juvenile vandalism. Have you broken up with any boyfriends lately? Stolen anyone else's boyfriend? Anything like that?"

"Not that I can think of," Abbie said, even though the name *Joey* was practically screaming to get out. I don't know it was Joey, she told herself firmly. But I intend to find out. I will do a little more investigating on my own and one way or another I will figure it out.

Today.

She bit her lip thoughtfully, looking around at the mess in her room.

And I know exactly what I'm going to do.

# Chapter 15

"Well." The fingerprint technician looked up from her work. "There's no point in bothering with the equipment at the lab."

"What do you mean?" Abbie looked ruefully at the blackish-grayish dust that had been carefully brushed over all the surfaces in her room. It's a total disaster in here! she thought. What the intruder didn't mess up, the cops did.

"I'm not dusting the things that were obviously not disturbed, but still, the only prints I'm finding are yours. I take it your parents and brother didn't come in here very often?"

Abbie shook her head. "Not really. It's my room."

"I know. I'm not faulting you. It's just that there are no other prints. We don't even need samples from the rest of the family because there's nothing else to identify."

"Thanks, anyway." So what did I expect?

Abbie thought. An instant solution? The guy leaves prints, the cops identify them, and all is fine?

"No problem." The woman packed her equipment. "You'd be surprised about prints," she said cheerfully. "I come, I dust, I compare. But it's pretty rare that I ever get anything useful, especially in a case like this."

After the woman left, Abbie surveyed her room.

"My room!" she said, clenching her teeth. "My things! Oh! My favorite sweater!" She held it in her hands, rubbing the fabric with her fingers. It reeked of mixed perfumes. Makeup smears were embedded in the fibers. Ruined, she thought. The dry cleaner will never be able to get this out.

She gathered all the strewn and scattered makeup- and perfume-spattered clothing that was washable and put it in the washing machine. She got the vacuum and a bucket of soapy water and scrubbed and polished, trying to erase all signs — all *feel* — of the intruder. She even moved her furniture and vacuumed behind it, stripped the bed of the bedding she hadn't used in the bathroom last night, and made it up with fresh sheets.

And all the time she cleaned, she fumed and raged, furious that someone had dared to do this. "It's so dirty!" she said out loud, trying to define what being invaded made her feel. "It's scary, mean, filthy, intrusive . . . it's awful!"

Taylor called, and Abbie filled her in on what had happened, adding, "I have to be here when the glass company comes, but I'm not going to school after that. I have something to do. I may not know much about what's going on, but I know one thing I'm going to do."

"What? Abbie, whatever it is, let me do it with you."

"Do you feel like taking a trip to Joey's house?"

"What are you going to do at his house? What did you find in his truck?"

Briefly, Abbie explained that she'd returned the keys unused.

"Don't you think you should look in the truck first? That was your plan, remember?"

"I don't have a way to get in the truck, remember?"

"George helped once," Taylor said. "Why not again?"

"I think Joey knows I got into his locker. I don't think we can count on him leaving the keys in there again. I think the best way to avoid running into Joey is to go to his house. If his truck's not parked outside, I'm going in."

"Then I'll meet you there."

"The glass people are coming at one o'clock," Abbie said. She figured quickly, allowing time to do the repair, then to run over to Joey's house. "Let's try for 2:15 at his place," she suggested. "If you're sure you want to join in. We'll have less than half an hour to explore before he gets home after school, but that should be enough."

At 2:15 Abbie jogged up to Joey's house. With any luck, she thought, he'll mess around awhile after school and not get home right away.

A few minutes later, Taylor appeared. "This walking stuff is for the birds," she said. "In the future, let's plan these things for when we have a car."

"I hardly think everything works that smoothly," Abbie said.

"How are we going to do this?" Taylor asked, gazing at the house. "What if the door's locked? What if someone's home?"

"We act like we belong," Abbie said, marching up the walk. Taylor scurried after her.

Abbie rang the doorbell, and when a woman answered, Abbie smiled.

"Hi," Abbie said brightly. "Joey left his notes for school on his dresser, and I said I'd pick them up for him."

"Oh." The woman looked vaguely perplexed. "How nice." She invited them in with a gesture, then pointed up a flight of stairs. "The first door. I'm right in the middle of a conference call, so if you don't mind . . ."

"Not at all," Abbie said, charging up the stairs. Taylor followed, making little alarmed noises of protest under her breath. The woman went back to her work, and Abbie paused outside the first door she came to.

"Here goes nothing," Abbie said, pushing the door.

"Wait!" Taylor said, clutching at her sleeve. "Let's go back. I'm scared."

"Of what?"

"I don't know. I just feel awful about this. My heart is pounding. It just doesn't feel right."

"I thought you didn't believe in premonitions," Abbie said.

"I don't. I don't. It's just . . . "

"I'm going in. You can go home if you want." Abbie pushed the door open and stood frozen in the doorway, shocked into silence by what she saw.

"This is insanity," she said finally.

And then she stepped into the room.

# Chapter 16

"This is so bizarre!" Abbie said, turning, unable to bring herself to go farther into the room, or to touch anything.

Everywhere she looked, she smiled down on herself. The room was huge, obviously a converted attic, and Abbie filled every wall. Poster-size photographs of herself — more than fifty of them — dominated with the smaller spaces filled in with eight-by-ten-inch shots. Wallet-size pictures were tacked up in any odd leftover spots.

"Look!" Taylor pointed, but Abbie had already noticed the place above Joey's bed, where a headboard would have been if the bed had had one. Instead, pinned to the wall over a life-size print of Abbie, positioned to look as if she were wearing it, was one of her missing sweatshirts.

"This is incredible!" said Taylor. "Look. He had a calendar made with you on every month."

Abbie looked, but didn't move.

"He's got a Mac computer, like at school," Taylor said. She turned the machine on.

"What are you doing?" Abbie asked.

"Being nosy," Taylor said. "Isn't that what we came here for? I begged you to leave and you wouldn't. So . . . as long as I'm here, I'm looking." She rattled her fingers over the keys. "Aha! We have a file named 'Abbie.' Should I peek?" She answered her own question by calling up the file. "Oh, my!" she said. "You are such a romantic, Abbie. I didn't know."

"What do you mean?"

"Just listen. 'Her hair is glorious in the sunshine, shining like copper. Her skin is so soft under my fingers. I remove my hand from her arm and wrap my fingers in her curls. I bring her face close to mine. Her eyes close and our lips touch. Abbie is mine. She whispers that she loves me, and . . . ' "

"Turn it off!" Abbie said.

"But it gets better!"

"I said turn it off!"

Taylor looked startled and hurt, but she exited the file and turned the machine off.

"Can he tell you got into his computer?" Abbie asked.

Taylor shrugged. "If he knows enough about computers and decides to look, I suppose he can. So? I thought you didn't care if he found out you were here. His mother will describe you."

Abbie shook her head helplessly. "I . . . " she said. "I never guessed what we'd find. This is creepy."

Taylor walked over to Joey's closet and opened the doors.

"No!" Abbie said. "We're leaving. Come on, Taylor. Now!"

Taylor started to protest, but Abbie turned and walked out of the room, down the stairs and outside, not even caring whether Taylor was behind her or not. Her stomach churned, and her head pounded.

She heard the front door of Joey's house close, but she didn't turn around to see whether it was Taylor or Joey's mother. Instead, she took off, trotting at first, then jogging aimlessly, paying no attention to her route.

She thought she heard someone yell, "Hey!" but she didn't care, didn't listen. She needed to be alone. She did not want to sit around and discuss what she'd just seen.

Joey's room had disturbed her.

It's like I wasn't real, she thought. I was pinned up all over like a specimen of some kind, like in a biology lab.

Even as she ran, Abbie shuddered, overwhelmed by the experience of Joey's room. She couldn't come to a conclusion, couldn't decide what she felt, except for torn apart, horrified, shook up and, strangest of all — she even felt sympathy. For Joey.

I invaded his room, she thought. I know what that feels like, and even if Joey did it to my room, I still shouldn't have done it to his.

She finally stopped running. She looked for a landmark to tell her where she was, but she didn't recognize anything. There were brand-new houses, most of them with only dirt for landscaping, many still under construction. She loped to a corner, looking for a street sign. There wasn't one.

Abbie sighed. I've managed to lose myself, she thought. She chose a house where two little girls in bright sweaters tossed a ball back and forth in the drive. Two tricycles littered the sidewalk.

She waved to the girls as she headed up the sidewalk.

"Hi," one little girl said. "You the Oats lady."

Abbie looked closer, then laughed as she recognized the daughter of a frequent customer at the health food store. "Yes. I'm Abbie. I'm going to ask your mom if I can use your phone."

"Oh, yes, you can," the girl said confidently. "It's in the kitchen. I talk to my friends sometimes."

Abbie smiled. "So do I," she said, knocking.

The woman who answered the door recognized Abbie, too.

Abbie explained about being lost. "I just need directions," she said. "I don't remember this neighborhood at all."

"It's no wonder. This was all field until a few months ago. We were one of the first families to move in. I don't quite understand, though. I thought you must have come for your car."

"What?" Abbie asked.

"Isn't that your car? Parked over there?" The woman came out on the porch, pointed toward a bulldozer. "Behind that machine. I'm sure it's yours because I see it at the shop and the numbers are . . . used to be the same as my phone. I thought maybe it'd broken down.

I've been kind of keeping an eye on it, waiting for you."

Abbie stood, staring, not believing. She took a few steps nearer, then ran, knelt, and examined the license plate of her stepmother's Subaru. The numbers reassured her. She'd found her stolen car!

And it looked fine. There was no sign of damage.

Abbie had her car keys, since they were on the ring with her house keys. She reached for the door handle, then jerked her hand back, thinking of the fingerprint technician and her shiny dust.

"Could I use your phone?" she asked.

She phoned the police department and explained her situation. The man who answered didn't seem impressed that she'd found the missing car, and only when Abbie threatened to drive the car home and mess up any prints that might be there did he agree to send someone out right away.

Right away turned out to be over an hour, but Abbie spent it happily, drinking black decaf tea with the Positive Oats customer and discussing antioxidants, fiber, how to avoid refined sugar, and the joy of fresh fruits and vegetables.

Abbie left with several new recipes, feeling a kinship that only seemed possible with other health food believers. Smiling, she met the police officer and the same fingerprint technician who'd left her house a few hours before.

Abbie gave her report to the officer while the technician went to work. They finished at the same time.

The technician shook her head. "Unlocked," she said. "And wiped clean."

The officer shrugged. "You're luckier than most. Usually the car is taken out of state, stripped, and sold for parts. Parts are worth more than the car itself is. You got your car back. Forget about who took it, and drive it home."

Abbie took his advice, parking in the garage where she could keep it safe behind locked doors.

Brett wasn't home yet, so Abbie started making a thick vegetable soup. While the soup simmered, she called Taylor.

"I'm sorry I ditched you," Abbie said. "It was just too much, Taylor. First my room gets trashed . . . then all those pictures of me in Joey's room. I couldn't take another second or I'd have flipped out. But I'm sorry I just ran off."

There was a long pause. It seemed, in the

years of her relationship with Taylor, that they took turns angering the other, sometimes over something small and petty, sometimes over bigger issues.

Every time Taylor truly angered her, or she truly angered Taylor, Abbie wondered if this was the time they had stepped over the line, the time when the friendship wouldn't be strong enough to survive the chasm.

Finally Taylor said, "You were pretty bizarre, Abbie. I just never know with you. You were determined to go to his house, you were convinced you had to do this, and you insisted on going in, even when I suggested backing off."

"I know."

"And then, just when we're finding all this information that might help, you get weird and leave. And you ditch me!"

"I know. But can you imagine if it had been you plastered all over those walls?"

"I have been imagining it," Taylor said. "That's why I forgive you. And I know it works both ways. I know you'd forgive me, too, if I did something weird. What I really want to know is, what are you doing tonight? For sleeping? To protect your room? Do I have to worry about you, or can I go on my date in peace?"

"Date?"

"Didn't I tell you? Ryan — you know. From the movies and coffee the other night? We're going out. He seems pretty nice."

"Umm . . . I barely remember those guys," Abbie admitted.

"Ryan was the one with dark hair and green eyes," Taylor explained. "The one who kept talking about his dog."

"Mmmm," Abbie said, but since she hadn't paid attention to the conversation that night, she still had no clue which one Taylor meant.

"Anyway, I thought that was really cute," Taylor went on. "I mean, most guys brag about themselves, or talk about cars or sports or other women, and here's Ryan talking about his new puppy. I liked that. So I gave him my phone number, and he called. I can't believe I didn't tell you this."

"I've been a little preoccupied with other things," Abbie pointed out.

"Yeah," Taylor said. "So, anyway, Brett can keep his good looks and his swimming muscles. I always figure an active interest is much better than a maybe, any old day."

"Absolutely," Abbie agreed.

"Look, I've got to go," Taylor said abruptly. "I have to get ready. Just reassure me you'll be safe tonight."

"I was fine last night," Abbie said. "I suppose I'll be fine tonight, too. I can't guarantee my bedroom will survive the night, but I will."

After she hung up, Abbie mixed up a batch of fat-free applesauce muffins, slid the pan into the oven, set the timer, and wondered if she *would* be safe overnight. If the first night someone had broken her bedroom window, and the second night someone had trashed her room, what would the third night bring?

On the other hand, the police had now been called into the case, and the attacker had probably seen the police car at the house. Abbie's mood began to brighten. There was a good chance that her stalker would be scared away for good.

The timer on the stove went off, and Abbie got up to turn off the oven. As she pulled out the muffin tray, something in the corner of her eye caught her attention. She snapped her head around, focusing.

The answering machine light.

Blinking.

Was it good news or bad news?

Abbie forced her feet to move to the machine, forced her shaking finger to reach out.

She pushed the button.

"It's not over yet," said a voice.

Then the machine went silent.

# Chapter 17

Abbie pushed the repeat button.

"It's not over yet."

The four words hadn't changed, didn't change no matter how many times Abbie pushed repeat.

She listened over and over, trying to identify the voice, to read something — anything, even hatred or anger — into the tone of voice, trying to believe she hadn't heard the message, that it wasn't real.

But it was real.

"It's not over yet."

So what is "it"? Abbie wondered. A joke? Let's terrorize Abbie week? A real person with a real grudge, or just someone trying to get their kicks by scaring me? Am I truly in danger for my life? That's just too hard to believe. I'm nobody. Why would anyone want to hurt me?

Get a grip! she told herself firmly. Focus on the task at hand — dinner.

She rescued the muffins and stirred the soup. The aroma of both reached inside her, soothed her with the smell of good, fresh food, of home and love and family. Without waiting for Brett, she dished herself up a bowl of soup, plopped two muffins on a plate, and sat down to eat.

She felt much better by the time Clif called, felt good enough that she could reassure him. "Last night was not good," she admitted. "But I was safe. And I'll be safe tonight. Maybe we can do something after school tomorrow. . . . I have to be to work at seven o'clock. Tonight, I need to deal with things around here."

After she hung up, Abbie examined her room. Whoever had broken in last night had used a hammer to pry off the boards Brett had nailed up.

The boards are in the shed, Abbie thought. I could get them and nail them up again on the inside of my room. Would that help? No, because the attacker could break the glass again and pound the boards into my room.

*It's not over yet.*

Is it Joey? Or is it someone else?

She hadn't decided by the time Brett came

home, and she didn't ask his opinion.

He was delighted she'd found the car, but that didn't stop his direct route to the kitchen. "Smells good," he said, lifting the lid on the soup.

Abbie watched anxiously as he ate, pleased that he scarfed three bowls of soup and five muffins, ate the meal eagerly without once asking if this was some of her fanatic super-healthy fiber-loaded food . . . which it was.

"I asked all around today," Brett announced, pushing his empty bowl away. "Nobody knows anything."

Abbie sighed. Nobody in his group. But who expected his group to know anything about someone who broke windows and terrorized people?

"Listen to this," Abbie said, replaying the message.

Brett clenched his fists. "Don't you think it's time we called the folks?"

Abbie kicked her chair. "No!" she shouted, surprising herself. "What can they do? They can't do anything except be upset. They'd be just as helpless as we are, and it would ruin their vacation on top of everything else. They couldn't even get home until tomorrow, even if they took the first plane out."

"It might be a good idea just having more

people around," Brett said. "And besides, they might have some good ideas. It's their house, Abbie. They should be told if something's wrong."

Abbie slumped in her chair, knowing he was right. But she hated the thought of calling them, explaining that she and Brett couldn't keep the house together for even three weeks, that they were failures.

"They never had a honeymoon," Abbie wailed. "They thought we were too young to leave when they got married, so they took us along. This is their first time alone together, without us. They deserve it! I don't want to ruin it for them. Do you?"

"Which is worse?" Brett asked. "Having your honeymoon ruined but saving your house and children, or finding out about everything when it's too late?"

"Okay." Abbie admitted defeat. "Call."

She left the kitchen, went outside. The day was gone and night had fallen, but she could still see well enough to stare blankly at her window, half a story up, the new glass winking darkly in the dusk.

How had the intruder reached the window last night? Did he get the ladder from the shed again? Or did he bring his own? If he got it from the shed, he put it back . . . and if he comes tonight, he'll expect to use it again. Why make it easy?

She ran inside and grabbed her keys, took the Subaru from the garage, and drove to the hardware store for a lock and hasp for the shed. At home, Brett held the flashlight and she installed the lock, pocketing the keys.

Anything to slow him down, she thought. "At least he'll have to supply his own tools," she said smugly.

"Mom and Dad weren't in," Brett said. "I left a message at the desk, but I guess they're off on a several-day inter-island cruise. The desk clerk wasn't too clear on which day they'd be back."

The night had grown sharply colder. "We'll have to do what we can by ourselves," she said.

"Yeah," Brett agreed. "Funny how I couldn't wait for them to be gone, and now I wish like everything they were here."

"I know. They're such bothers, till they're gone."

"So," Brett said as they headed into the house, "the bathroom fortresses again tonight?"

Abbie shook her head. "Not for me. I'm not going to sleep. I'm going to keep watch."

"Then I will, too," Brett said.

"Thanks," Abbie told him. "Do you have any good ideas how to go about this? Leave all the house lights on, I suppose."

"Yeah. And we have that portable light Dad uses in the garage. It's got a hook on it. We could run an extension cord and hang it near your window somewhere."

Abbie grabbed a sweatshirt from the closet.

"You're going to need more than that!" Brett said. "It's supposed to be near freezing tonight."

"Right. A coat, a sleeping bag, a couple of flashlights, a thermos of tea, some food . . . well, we won't need to take everything outside. We can go in and out of the house. We don't have to stay outside every minute."

She paused. "Let's just be sure we lock the door, though. Even when we're in the house, let's keep the door locked."

Brett nodded. "Do you want the front yard or the back?"

Abbie stuffed her arms through the sweatshirt sleeves and grabbed her coat. "Back. I'm going to watch my window. Let's get that light set up."

They reopened the shed, and with the help of the ladder, hammer and nails, and two long extension cords, they managed to rig the portable light so it hung near Abbie's window and lit the area below it. Then they relocked the shed.

Abbie carried out her camping equipment and set it up in the backyard, where she could see the rear of the house.

She got into the down-filled sleeping bag and pulled up the zipper.

Then she lay back to watch . . . and wait.

# Chapter 18

At first, it was easy to stay awake. Anger, determination, and hot tea combined with the chilly October night temperatures to keep Abbie on edge and alert to every movement and every noise.

But each disturbance turned out to be windblown bushes, the neighborhood cats, a confused and sleepy bird. Abbie began to drowse. The occasional traffic going by began to sound like the drone of late summer, and Abbie found herself jerking awake.

Maybe I should get up and move around a little, she thought, stumbling out of her sleeping bag. She patrolled the rear of the house, then each side, finding nothing out of the ordinary.

That front light is really not bright enough, Abbie thought as she rounded the corner of the house. We should have put in a brighter bulb.

Abbie stopped, playing her flashlight across the front of the house.

What was that? On the porch.

Abbie's breath came faster and she took a cautious step forward.

It looked like a body.

Abbie's heart pounded, and she could hear blood rushing in her ears. Slowly she forced herself toward the porch.

As she neared the body, Abbie saw it was encased in a sleeping bag, with even the head covered. It was Brett. But why was his head covered?

Something rustled behind her.

Spooked, she whipped her head around, looking, but no one sprang up with a knife.

"Brett?" she called. "Are you all right?"

There was no reply.

"Brett?" she called again.

Still no answer.

She crept up on the porch, reached out a hand . . . and the sleeping bag moved.

Abbie screamed.

Brett pulled the bag away from his face and blinked sleepily at her. "What's the matter?"

"I thought you were dead." Abbie sat down abruptly, afraid her knees would give out.

"Just cold," Brett said grumpily. "I didn't mean to go to sleep. I just wanted to warm up." He pulled his arms free of the bag. "I was guarding the door, anyway," Brett said, pushing the bag down over his legs.

Abbie took a deep breath and let it out. "I'm going to make some coffee," she told him.

"Coffee? You?" Brett asked, flinging the sleeping bag aside. "Real coffee? Are you serious?"

"I was having trouble staying awake."

"Me, too, obviously."

Abbie grinned. "I thought the caffeine might help keep me awake. Will you check the house while I make the coffee?"

"Sure. Especially if you make a few sandwiches, too."

Abbie made thick ham-and-cheese sandwiches for Brett, and a whole-grain, low-fat cream cheese and apple sandwich for herself. She filled a thermos with coffee for each of them.

They stationed themselves at their posts again.

Abbie finished her coffee at two-thirty. Restless and jumpy, she wandered back and forth across the lawn, in and out of shadows. She leaned against the shed in the dark and watched the brightly lit area near her window.

The caffeine throbbed in her head, aching, making her lightheaded. But at the same time she had an urgent need to keep moving.

I should know better than to drink caffeine! she thought, pacing to the edges of the yard, first to the left, then to the right. This is so boring! Stakeouts never look this boring on TV!

At 3:15 she checked on Brett. He was asleep again, this time propped up against the front door with his sleeping bag cocooned around him. A light, rhythmic snore rumbled across the air between them.

Abbie increased her patrol to the full three sides of the house, peering across the front yard each time, too, just before she reversed directions.

The minutes ticked by, crawling, and the darkness widened and deepened. An occasional breath of wind rattled tree branches, dried and drying leaves scuttling each other like rat claws.

Once in a while she could hear a car driving by out front and she envied the drivers, for they had somewhere to go and someone to see.

She returned to the shed and sat down, leaning against it. An aching loneliness sprang from the dark and settled in Abbie's chest. She wrapped herself in her sleeping bag, hugging it around her.

You've been alone before, she chided herself.

She looked around, looked at the silent black shapes of nearby houses and told herself she was in the midst of a crowd of people. And Brett was still sleeping just a few yards away.

But it didn't help. The aloneness sat like ice in her chest, cold and hard and comfortless.

*And someone's after me. Someone wants to hurt me, and I don't know who. I don't know why.*

A distant siren wailed, the noise carrying in eerie waves. Then, from closer, "Mrrow?"

"Oh, Toast! Hello!" Abbie told the cat. "Took you long enough to come visiting." The cat rubbed against the sleeping bag. Abbie scratched Toast's head, behind the ears. "Are you out hunting?"

Toast purred, pressing her head into Abbie's hand.

"So am I, kind of," Abbie said. "Hunting . . . or trying to keep from being hunted. Something like that."

Toast took the attention as an invitation and leaped onto the sleeping bag.

"I don't know how you amuse yourself all night long," Abbie said. "I'm bored stiff. And cold."

Off in the distance a phone rang.

"Bad news for someone," Abbie murmured. "No one calls in the middle of the night unless it's bad news."

She counted five rings before the phone stopped. In a few minutes it started again. "Actually . . . " Abbie stood up, the cat jumping sideways to avoid being toppled. "That sounds like . . . it's coming from my room!"

Abbie raced over and stood in the light beneath her window. The ringing was louder. It was definitely coming from her room, but it stopped as she stood there. Five rings.

Their answering machine was set to answer on the sixth ring.

Will they call again? Should I go in and wait?

She headed toward the front door, then stopped. She bit her lip, thinking. Was someone trying to lure her into the house? Could it be a trick?

She looked at her watch . . . 4:15 A.M. *Two more hours and I'll be getting up. I can do normal, everyday things again instead of prowling around in my own yard. I can shower, I can go to school . . . oh, no! It's Friday tomorrow. Today, I mean. I have to go to school all day, and then I have to work at the shop all evening! After no sleep. I'll be dead!*

The thought echoed, as if it had been spoken aloud.

"I'll be dead. Dead."

# Chapter 19

The rest of the night passed uneventfully, and almost before she knew it, Abbie was on her way to school.

She looked longingly at the garage door, but shook her head. Whoever stole her mother's car could just do it again, she thought. And it might not be so easy to find next time.

She checked that the garage door was locked, and headed for school, but as soon as she got there she wanted to turn around and go home again, to make sure things were okay. Stop! she ordered herself, leaning against a tree on the school grounds. Just calm down.

Besides, she thought. I'm probably safer at school than anywhere else. There are so many people around. Nobody would dare do anything to me in such a public place.

Taylor hurried over, full of news, gushing about Ryan.

Ryan? Abbie thought. Then she remembered. Taylor's date.

"We stopped by his place to see the puppy. . . ."

Abbie listened politely, corralling her attention when it wandered, making little noises of interest now and then. When the first bell rang, she nudged Taylor toward the front door of the school, but halfway there Taylor stopped, gesturing again. When Abbie realized there were only seconds till the final bell, she grabbed Taylor by the arm and hauled her inside. "Hurry," she said. "We'll be late."

"My book's in the locker," Taylor protested.

"You'll have to share. Hurry!" They'd barely cleared the doorway when the final bell rang and the teacher glared.

"I'm glad you had a good time," Abbie whispered, slipping off her sweatshirt-jacket. She draped it over the back of her chair and got to work on the day's assignment. In a minute, the quiet click of computer keys filled the room.

When she'd finished typing her work, Abbie sent it to the printer and watched the screen for the "PRINTING" message to flash. There were only five printers for the class, so there was usually a wait.

She heard footsteps pause at her chair, and looked up into Joey's yearning face.

The pictures in his room flashed in front of Abbie's eyes.

"Mom said a redhead," Joey said. It was almost an apology. His hands fingered her sweatshirt-jacket on the back of her chair, twisting the fabric.

Abbie watched, fascinated, as he stroked and rubbed, unable to leave the jacket alone. "You have one at home," she said.

Joey yanked his hands away, his face burning. The jacket slid to the floor. "Sorry!" Joey knelt, gathering up the jacket.

This is so awkward, Abbie thought, as Joey hung her jacket back on the chair. He jammed his hands into his pockets, maybe hoping that would keep them away from her jacket.

"Mr. Mowry?" the teacher asked. "Do you have a problem?"

Joey gulped. He shook his head, shooting a pleading look at Abbie as he hurried to the printers and tore off his sheets.

I can't believe Joey is the one terrorizing me, Abbie thought. But who else could it be? He seems so helpless. Her screen was finally flashing the "PRINTING" message, but she waited until Joey was back in his seat before she retrieved her pages.

After class, ignoring Joey's tentative "Abbie, can we talk?", Abbie grabbed Taylor's arm, brushed past Joey, and steered Taylor toward their lockers in the senior hall.

"What did you say to Joey?" Taylor asked.

"Nothing," Abbie said.

"What about last night? What happened?"

"Nothing," Abbie said.

"Fine, don't tell me." Taylor waved at some guys passing by. "Just pretend like I'm not here."

Abbie sighed.

"I stayed up all night, outside, watching," Abbie said. "And nothing happened. I think Joey wanted to talk, but I said nothing to him."

"Oh, I see," Taylor said, nodding. "Nothing and nothing. You weren't just putting me off."

Abbie spun her locker combination. Then she yanked the door open so hard, it banged against the next locker and slammed shut again.

Taylor looked shocked. "You need a vacation," she said, gently opening her own locker door. "You are under way too much strain. How many nights do you think you can go without sleep?"

Abbie leaned her head against the cool metal door. "Maybe I can catch a nap this afternoon," she said. "Except I told Clif we'd do something after school."

She dialed her combination again, then carefully and deliberately lifted the latch and opened the door.

She looked inside the locker.

Then, just as deliberately, just as carefully, she turned and walked off, leaving Taylor staring openmouthed at Abbie's open locker.

Inside, a photo of Abbie hung suspended on a string. The eyes, the throat, and other pieces of the picture had been slashed away.

"Abbie!" Taylor called. "Did you see?"

Abbie just kept walking. I know who's responsible for this, she thought, her eyes searching the halls. And I'm going to find him. I'm going to get him.

I will get him.

# Chapter 20

George stood with his hands out, palms up, warding her off. "I don't know!" he repeated. "I never pay attention. I don't remember."

"You DO know!" Abbie insisted. "If you opened my locker in the past twenty-four hours, you would remember. So just tell me!"

"I open ten lockers a day. Twenty! And it's my policy to forget. You know that. I told you. How long do you think I would last if I told? How would you like it if I told everyone I'd opened lockers for you?"

"One locker," Abbie snapped. "And I don't care if you tell. Did you open my locker for someone? Today? Just nod your head for yes; shake it for no."

"I don't remember," George said again. He said it slowly and firmly. "Do you understand me? I CAN tell you nothing and I WILL tell you nothing."

"I'll tell the principal," Abbie threatened, wincing inside at the childishness of the words.

"Go ahead. I'll deny everything."

"Taylor saw you, too."

"So? I can guarantee you, I'll have an alibi. You can't prove anything. Give it up." George pushed his way between Abbie and Taylor and strode off.

"I guess that didn't work," Abbie said bleakly as they walked back to her locker. She spun the dial a third time, took a deep breath, and let it out as she opened the locker door.

Abbie looked at the picture of herself one more time, then reached out and pulled it from the string. She yanked the books down that she would need for the rest of the morning classes.

"Thanks for sticking with me," she told Taylor. "I'm sorry. I've made you late for class." She juggled her books, sliding them into her bag. "See you at lunch."

Taylor made a face. "I have to retake my math test at lunch. Either that or be happy with a D-minus. And I'm seeing Ryan after school."

"I think I'm doing something after school, too," Abbie told her. "So I'll just call you later if we don't meet up."

They headed separate ways and, since she

was late, Abbie hurried. She dashed into class, glad to see people still milling around, visiting while the teacher wrote the day's important points on the board. Abbie slid into her seat, grabbed her English book and notebook from her bag, and was ready when the teacher turned around to take attendance.

Abbie peered past her at the board. "Graded class discussion. Myth versus legend. Heroes and antiheroes. What drives the hero?" Okay, Abbie thought. I can do this. I can think about English. I can participate in class discussions.

Abbie did a good job taking part in the discussion until midway through the class when she noticed a little corner of paper protruding from her book. She pulled it out, looked at it.

There, in the same style of cutout magazine letters as before, was the message:

ITS NOT OVER U C IM KRAZY

She dropped the note on her desk, feeling a scream of frustration, rage, and fear welling up in her throat. She clapped her hands over her mouth to keep it in.

"Ms. Grant, are you all right?"

Abbie shook her head no.

"You're excused," said the teacher.

Abbie shoved everything back inside her

pack and, keeping one hand over her mouth, rushed out of the room, out of the building, off to the far corner of the parking lot. There, she did scream. Then she sank onto the curb and held her head in her hands, drawing in huge gulps of fresh air.

ITS NOT OVER U C IM KRAZY

He didn't finish the message, she thought numbly.

Unless the message has changed.

IM KRAZY

I feel like I've had a whole pot of coffee, Abbie thought, jumping up, pacing. I have to DO something and I don't know what.

She was dimly aware of a blue pickup truck turning into the student lot, driving along the lines of cars, but it didn't really register until it drove up and stopped right in front of her. Then she focused on it.

Joey.

He rolled down his window. "Aren't you cold? Where's your jacket?"

Abbie looked around. "I must have left it in English."

"Do you want me to go get it?"

Abbie shook her head. She remembered his hands caressing it in computer lab and, as if he could read her mind, Joey flushed. "Could we talk, Abbie?" he asked. "Please? It's warmer in here."

I guess we really need to do this, Abbie thought. "Drive over there and park," she told him.

Joey obeyed.

Abbie followed. "Give me the keys."

When he'd handed them over, Abbie grabbed her pack and tossed it on the seat so it would be between them. She climbed in.

"Look," Abbie said bluntly. "You've got to leave me alone. You've got to get over this."

"I never thought you'd see my room," Joey mumbled. "I never would have done that if I'd thought you would see it. I never meant you to."

"Well, I did see it. It's pretty bad."

"No it's not," Joey said. "It's beautiful. It's . . . soothing. I look at you and I talk to you and I feel better."

"It's too much. It's sick, Joey. You're obsessed."

Joey looked indignant. "It happens to be perfectly normal for guys to be obsessed with girls!"

"Girls, plural," Abbie pointed out. "Not one girl, and not for years and years."

"I don't see anything wrong with it," Joey

insisted. "I love you, Abbie. You must know that. And I like having reminders of you around. But that's not what . . . "

Abbie, taking a chance, reached over and flipped down his sun visor. She looked pointedly at the snapshots of herself taped there. "I figured as much," she said.

Joey flushed again and looked down at his hands.

Abbie pressed the release button on the glove compartment. The door fell open.

Joey's lips compressed into a straight line, but he made no protest as she pulled out the polished wooden box, set it on her lap, and slipped the lid off.

"A pencil," she said, fingering it. "With my name on it. My bracelet! Where'd you get it?"

It wasn't much of a bracelet, just one she'd strung together in jewelry class once, green and white beads. She remembered choosing them, how her fingers had fumbled, then grown less awkward as she worked.

"What's this?" She unwrapped the paper, much-creased, almost falling apart. "Joey? This is a note I wrote to Taylor years ago!" She flushed, reading it. *I think Nick is pretty hot stuff. What do you think?*

When's the last time I even wrote someone

a note? she wondered, fingering the almost-shredded paper.

"And this?" She touched the purplish leaf and remembered Clif handing it to her — a world ago and in another world — remembered slipping it into the pocket of her sweat-shirt-jacket.

The same jacket that Joey had knocked to the floor in computer lab that morning.

"Joey!" she said. "You took this from my jacket pocket!"

"It's just a leaf! I didn't know it was something you wanted. I thought it had just fallen on you or something. I never thought you would notice it was gone."

Abbie shook her head, poking at the odd things in the box. "Explain," she demanded.

Joey wouldn't look at her, but he spoke, his voice wooden. "The rocks are from your driveway. That Band-Aid is from when you fell in the powder-puff football game. The shoelace piece is from when you were running cross-country that time and got a rock in your shoe and then the lace broke when you retied it."

"Oh, Joey!" Abbie couldn't think what to say. "Tell me the rest," she finally said.

"I'm afraid you're going to get hurt!" he blurted.

"That's why you're following me everywhere? To protect me?"

"Yes. I don't want . . . "

"I can't believe this! Joey, you are terrorizing me!"

"No. I'm trying to help you."

Abbie had had enough. She grabbed her pack and tossed his box of things onto the seat between them. "I don't need your kind of help. You're making me nuts! Just leave me alone!"

"But you're in danger!" Joey shouted. "You need me!"

"I need water, food, and shelter," Abbie shouted back, all sympathy gone. "I don't need you poking around in my room, leaving things in my locker, following me, calling me, threatening me. Leave me alone! Do you hear me?" She slid out of the truck.

"I'm not . . . it's not . . . I'm only trying to help. Don't you understand you're being threatened?"

"Oh, I understand all right," Abbie said. "You've made it quite clear." From her backpack, Abbie yanked the slashed picture she'd found in her locker. She threw it at Joey. "That kind of help I can do without!" she yelled. She turned and ran, ran blindly, not caring where she went.

She could hear Joey shouting after her, but

she ignored him. How can this be happening? she thought as she ran. What did I do to deserve this? Why me?

After a while she stopped, her initial burst of rage wearing off, leaving her drained. She turned, heading back to school.

I'm as safe there as I am anywhere, she thought. And I can't keep missing classes.

She sat alone at lunch — alone except for Joey, keeping watch from two tables away — and tried to come to some conclusions.

Joey is obsessed with me, she thought, mentally ticking off points. Someone is out to get me, Joey . . . or someone. Anyone could get into my locker if they paid George to do it. Taylor has my combination and wouldn't need George's help. Taylor knows which bedroom is mine, and she knew when I left her house that day I almost got ran over.

She stared at her carrot sticks while her mind kept going in circles. It could be anyone. I hate suspecting everyone, but it's stupid not to. Someone is doing this . . . and I don't even know what "this" is. Is someone playing a dumb game, trying to scare me? Or does someone actually want to hurt me?

Who?

And what can I do about it?

She raised her head and looked at Joey, met

his eyes. He flushed at her stare, but he didn't look away.

Where were you this morning? Abbie wondered. Why were you driving INTO the parking lot in the middle of the morning? Where were you coming from, and what were you doing there?

Abbie had a sudden, overwhelming urge to go home . . . and a sudden, overpowering fear of what she would find there.

# Chapter 21

The rest of the day dragged by.

Abbie was nearly frantic to get home by the time the last bell rang, releasing her. She ran to her locker, fingers fumbling as she spun the dial.

Her stomach tensed.

I'm afraid to open my locker! she thought. She took a deep breath and started over, more slowly.

I will take everything out, she decided. I just won't use my locker any more. I can carry my books with me. I can carry my jacket . . . my jacket! Is it still in the English room?

She ignored her dread and yanked the locker door open. Everything seemed to be in order, but she was not relieved.

This just means the attack will happen somewhere else, she thought grimly. She pulled out all her books and notebooks, stuffed them in her backpack, and slammed the door.

"Hey," Clif greeted her.

"Hi." Abbie shouldered her pack.

"Are we still on for after school?"

"Sort of," Abbie said slowly. "It depends."

"Sort of?" Clif looked amused. "I never know what to expect from you, Abbie. What does 'sort of, it depends' mean?"

"I want to check my house," Abbie said. "If you want to skip that part and meet me later . . ."

"No way," Clif said. "You're stuck with me. Now fill me in. What was all that about your house being trashed and the police and all?"

Abbie explained as they left, stopping by the English room to collect her jacket.

"Abbie." Clif took her arm. "Don't go home."

"I have to."

"Why? Listen to me, Abbie. These attacks are happening at your house, your car, and your locker. You had the right idea when you decided not to drive the car and to quit using your locker. Why be silly? Don't go home."

"It's not that simple." Abbie waited for Clif to unlock his truck. "In the first place, it's my home. That's where I live. My things are there. My food is there. Brett is there. It's not that easy to just walk away and leave everything behind."

Clif opened the door, and Abbie climbed onto the seat, fastened her seat belt. "And in the second place," she said as he got in his side, "it's ME they're after. Not my locker, not the car, not even my room. ME. And I take myself wherever I go. That's just the way it works."

"Then we'll go together. You can pack some things so you won't be leaving everything behind, and come stay at my house."

"Your house? How will your parents like it when someone breaks your windows to get at me? Clif, I am trouble."

"You're *in* trouble," Clif said, slowing for a red light, then stopping. "Friends help friends when they're in trouble."

"I don't know." Abbie stared glumly out the window. "I'll think about it."

"Unless," Clif said softly, "unless you still think it's me doing all this."

"I never thought it was you, Clif. Not specifically," Abbie told him. "I don't think it's anybody. I mean, I don't know who it is. But it's someone. Do you see?"

"Yeah." Clif drove in silence for a while. "Well," he said finally. "I guess you're right.

As long as you agree to suspect everyone equally, I guess I don't mind being on the list."

Abbie grinned. I like him, she thought. *And I hope it's not him.*

Clif parked in front of her house, and they both saw the problem at the same time.

Abbie's front door was wide open.

"Is your brother home?" Clif asked.

Abbie shook her head. "He shouldn't be. Swim practice. His car's not here."

"Then this is not good. How do you want to handle it?" Clif asked.

I want to run away and hide, Abbie thought. "I'm going in," she said.

"I'm right behind you."

Abbie felt like a criminal entering her own house, pausing, listening to see if anyone was there, then taking a few more cautious steps before pausing again.

She made her way through the living room, the kitchen, and down the hall. Clif checked the bathroom as they passed, raising his eyebrows at the padlock hasp screwed to the door frame.

The door to her room was closed.

She reached out and took the knob in her hand.

"Do you want me to go first?" Clif whispered.

Abbie shook her head. How bad can it be? she thought. I've already seen it trashed. The only thing worse would be if there was a maniac in there, waiting with a knife. That would be bad.

I could send Clif to the kitchen for a butcher knife — but if Clif turns out to be the maniac, that would be very bad.

If there's no maniac, then I'm fine.

She turned the knob and pushed the door open.

# Chapter 22

"Don't touch anything!" Abbie ordered.

The only thing in the room that had been disturbed was the bed, and somehow, the contrast with her neat and orderly bedroom made the carnage on the bed seem even worse.

"It's me," Abbie said, looking at the slashed jeans and sweatshirt arranged so carefully on the slashed bedspread, arranged as if it were Abbie lying there. In the place where her head would be were hacked pieces of photos, chopped up pictures of Abbie, piled on a slashed pillow.

"What's that?" Clif pointed to the sweatshirt, to something hidden inside the slash where Abbie's heart would be.

Abbie leaned over, peering. "It looks like a piece of paper." She reached through the slash and pulled it out.

It read, in the same cutout letters as the other messages, "4 U."

"Well, at least he likes to finish what he started," Abbie said, tossing the paper back onto the bed.

"The rest of the message from this morning?"

Abbie nodded calmly enough, but her pulse raced and her hands were icy.

"I don't like this at all," Clif said. "I'd feel better if I checked around."

Abbie nodded. I would feel better, too, she thought. But I'm sure the prowler is gone. Whoever it is likes to work fast and get out.

Abbie backed out of her room. She had no desire to touch anything. Nothing in her room seemed like it belonged to her anymore. It belonged to the shadowy figure of the terrorist, who could go anywhere, do anything, invade any place he wanted.

I have nothing left, Abbie thought. My makeup, my clothes, my room, my house . . . nothing. I have nothing.

She slammed the door to her room. I will not fall apart, she chanted silently. I will not fall apart. I will be sane. I will take charge. I will be fine.

In the living room she picked up the phone

and called the police, eventually talking to the officers who had come out before.

Clif rejoined her, shaking his head. No one else was in the house.

The police arrived later, and, by then, Abbie could calmly show them the mess on her bed, pointing out the "4 U" note and the first half of the message in her backpack. She even smiled when they decided not to bother with fingerprints.

"It's probably the same person," the woman cop pointed out. "And there were no fingerprints before."

Abbie nodded. I'm going to die, she thought, smiling politely at the police officers. She felt unreal, as if maybe she didn't really exist. *I'm going to die and there's not a thing they can do about it.*

"We'll do a couple of extra patrols," the officers promised. "We know how frightening this must be for you, but you'll be okay."

"They think it's me," Abbie told Clif as they found a place to sit at the Burger Joint. "They think I'm staging this, making it look like someone is after me."

Clif handed her a menu, then suddenly slapped himself on the forehead. "What am I thinking!" he said. "You can't eat here!"

"I can always eat a salad," Abbie told him.

"It's okay, Clif. There are certain unwritten rules about being a fanatic. We are incredibly flexible. At least we are if we want to go anywhere with friends."

"I feel really stupid being hungry when everything's so nuts for you," Clif said. "But I am. I'm starved."

Abbie tried to smile. She wasn't sure if it worked.

She surprised herself by eating heartily, finishing everything she ordered. It's been an emotional day, she thought. Maybe emotions make me hungrier than I thought.

"So what are you going to do?" Clif asked, signaling the waiter for more tea.

Abbie shrugged, shaking her head. "I don't know what I'm going to do," she said. "My parents aren't due home for almost two more weeks . . . and I don't even know if having them home will be safer for me, or just put more people in danger. What can I do for two weeks?"

"Stay at my place."

"We've been through that already," Abbie said.

"I understand I'm on your list of suspects," Clif said. "But my parents can't be! What if I stayed somewhere else?"

Abbie rubbed her forehead with her palm,

feeling weary. "Clif, I can't think. I'm not even sure if thinking will help any. My mom always used to tell me to take ten deep breaths and sleep on it before I made an important decision, but I can't even sleep."

"Do you have any relatives? Could you drive somewhere out of state?"

Abbie shook her head. "What about school? I'm a senior. I'd like to graduate with my class. Even if I did have somewhere I could go, I'd never graduate if I missed two weeks of school."

"But if you're in danger . . . "

"That's the question," Abbie said slowly. "Everything that's happened, except for the broken window, happened when I was gone, when I was *not* in my room, or near my locker, or near the car."

"But if you'd been in your bedroom instead of sleeping in a locked bathroom, who knows what would have happened?"

"Maybe the intruder would have left a note and gone away without doing anything. Maybe my room was trashed *because* I wasn't in it."

Clif made a fist and very deliberately pounded the table, one time, hard. "We're guessing," he said. "And that's what is so frustrating. We don't know."

"We don't know anything," Abbie agreed. "Except that I am the one in trouble. So whatever I decide to do, I'll decide it alone, and I'll do it alone. I'm not bringing anyone else into this. It's bad enough for me, but I'd never forgive myself if someone else got hurt because of me."

Abbie stood, tossing her napkin onto her plate. "Thanks for dinner, Clif, and for being with me at the house. I think I'd better go now. Sometime today I will make some decisions, and when I do, maybe I'll know what I'm doing. I'll see you Monday at school, okay?"

Emotions flickered over Clif's face as he tried to think of something to say.

Abbie blew him a kiss and left.

The Burger Joint wasn't much farther from her house than the school was, so Abbie jogged home. She didn't go into the house, just unlocked the garage door and took the Subaru.

It was too early for work, so she drove toward Taylor's house. As she drove she thought back over her friend's behavior the past few days, looking for signs of guilt or innocence.

I feel like a jerk for suspecting Taylor, Abbie

thought. But I told Clif I had to suspect everyone equally . . . and I do have to do that if I'm going to survive.

So, arguments FOR Taylor being the one doing this stuff: she knows everything about me. And she certainly has lots of pictures of me she could have cut up.

And she was disturbed every time I mentioned my premonition.

Arguments AGAINST it being Taylor? She's been my best friend forever. Why would she want to hurt me?

"I'm not perfect," she muttered, making the turn onto Taylor's street. "But why would *anyone* want to hurt me? I'm just not the kind of person who has enemies. At least in all the books I've read, you've got to be something out of the ordinary to have enemies — really pretty, super popular, extra mean — something!"

She parked in front of Taylor's house and leaned her head against the side window, closing her eyes.

If I could only draw my attacker out into the open, she thought, maybe lure him. . . .

A sense of power swept over her.

Be careful, she warned herself. It's only an idea. It might not work.

But it didn't matter. If it didn't work, at least she had an idea, finally!

Maybe even a plan.

She got out of the car, humming, heading up the walk toward Taylor's door.

# Chapter 23

"You're cheerful," Taylor said, opening the door.

"Yes, I am." Abbie slipped off her sweat-shirt and tossed it on the couch.

"So what gives? Why are you smiling?"

"Is it so unusual?"

Taylor faced her squarely. "Lately, yes."

"You know what I've been going through," said Abbie. "I haven't had much to smile about."

"I suppose," Taylor said. She shrugged. "It's just that all those things that have happened to you are a little hard to believe. I mean, if someone came up to you and told you all the stuff that's going on, what would you say?"

Abbie plopped onto the couch. "I'd say they were crazy."

Taylor nodded.

"Is that what you think?" asked Abbie. "That I'm crazy?"

"I have to admit, the idea occurred to me that maybe you just wanted attention." Taylor disappeared into the kitchen, returning in a minute with a bowl of unbuttered air-popped popcorn, a can of Coke, and a mug of still-brewing tea. Black. Decaf.

That's a true friend, Abbie thought. Who else would keep plain popcorn around for just one person. And decaf tea. She hates it. She keeps it for me.

So it can't be Taylor who's after me, right?

"Sometimes I wonder how well we know anybody," Taylor said, examining her Coke can before taking a sip. "Take Ryan, for example."

Ryan? Abbie thought. Oh, the movies, coffee, the date. "Cute little puppy?"

"Right. I met him after school, and we went to his place to see the puppy. In the course of an hour I learned the puppy belongs to a neighbor, Ryan's little sister is dog-sitting, and Ryan has been feeding me lines. He knew there was a puppy at home and he played it for all it was worth. I fell for it. Today he showed a little more of his true colors. I didn't like them."

"Are you okay?" Abbie asked.

"Oh, sure," Taylor said bravely. "I'll get over him pretty fast."

Abbie hugged Taylor, and after a while Taylor sat down on the couch beside her.

"I went out with Clif," Abbie said. "From computer lab?"

"Clif Howard? He was your maybe?"

"Yeah. And we had fun, after the police left."

Taylor blinked, then gave Abbie a long, silent stare. "Do I want to know?"

"I don't know. Do you?"

Taylor stood up, paced to the window, and stared out. "When I was little," she said softly, "I knew things sometimes. I'd get — not like a picture, but a feeling. Like a quiet little voice inside that said 'don't go that way' or something silly like that.

"It was no big deal. I mean, if I got the feeling I should turn left, I turned left. I never went the other way, so I never knew what would happen if I did. See?"

Abbie nodded. "I wouldn't mind having a little voice that guided me. Especially right now."

"I thought everybody had one." Taylor turned away from the window, but she couldn't look at Abbie. "I didn't know my inner voice was different from anyone else's."

Taylor picked up some popcorn and stared at it before putting it back in the bowl. "When I was thirteen, I had some friends. They were older and a little wild, so naturally my parents hated them. And just as naturally, that made me want to be with them every second I could."

Abbie nodded. "Perfectly reasonable for a thirteen-year-old."

"So when they invited me to a party, of course I had to go." Taylor pushed the popcorn bowl aside. "I HAD to go," she repeated. "Even though my little voice said not to."

"Uh-oh," Abbie said. "And that was the first time you didn't listen?"

Taylor nodded. "Every time I thought about the party, I got all excited. Going to a party with older kids. No parents to make us go home early. Boys. It sounded like more fun that anything I could imagine. And my stupid little voice was telling me to stay home.

"So when Friday night came, I told Mom I was staying overnight at a friend's house — a friend she liked and approved of — and I walked a couple of blocks over to where my friends were going to pick me up."

She paused again for a long time, wiping her hands over and over with her napkin. "Nobody ever told me what happens when you don't listen to the voice," she said, twisting the napkin until it tore.

"There was a terrible car accident. I couldn't deal with it. Two of my friends DIED, Abbie. I will never forget one single detail about that night. It was the most horrible night of my life."

Taylor sank to the floor, scattering popcorn and napkins, weeping. "My voice told me not to go. I knew! I didn't want to know anymore. I blocked out the voice!"

Abbie sank down next to her friend, hugging her. "Taylor, it's okay," she murmured.

"I could have lived with the accident and the deaths," Taylor said, sobbing. "It would have been hard, but I could have done it, if I just hadn't KNOWN. That makes it my fault, see? Because I should have stopped everyone from going."

"Oh, Taylor! You can't be responsible for an accident."

"If someone says don't do it, and you do it, and something bad happens, it's your fault. Maybe I could have stopped the accident by not going." Taylor used the scattered napkins to wipe her eyes and cheeks.

Abbie remembered Taylor's earlier remark about Ryan — *How well do we know anybody?*

How well, indeed? she thought. As long as

we've been friends, I never knew about this. "I'm so sorry," she murmured. "But you can't know the accident wouldn't have happened, anyway. The only difference might have been that you weren't in the car."

"If I had even told them, warned them, they might have stayed home. I didn't even do that."

That explains why she didn't want to hear about my premonition, Abbie thought. And now I feel like an idiot. I've been resenting my best friend for not supporting me in my problem. And all the time, the real problem was that every time I said the word *premonition*, I reminded her of the accident.

Are we all haunted? Does everybody have ghosts from the past?

"Taylor?" Abbie said. "I'm not just trying to get attention."

"I know," Taylor said, her eyes still dark and blank. "Abbie . . ."

"What?"

"Don't go."

"What?"

"Wherever you're going," Taylor said. "Don't go."

# Chapter 24

I have to go, Abbie thought. I have to go to work. It's the perfect place to lure someone when you don't know who it is. I'll be alone because I'm closing tonight. I don't have much of a plan, but what little I have means I have to go to work.

"Please?" Taylor said. Her eyes focused on Abbie. "It's the voice. I can hear it."

"I'll be careful," said Abbie. "But I have to do it."

"Do what?" Taylor shivered.

"Just go to work, that's all. Then home to sleep in my own bed in my own house."

After leaving Taylor's house, Abbie thought about her plan. It's simple, really, she thought. I've got to get this person to make a move, which means I have to do all my normal stuff, at the normal times. No more hiding.

Abbie stopped at a little strip shopping mall

on the way to work. At a hobby shop, she bought a child-size wooden baseball bat. At a little gas-and-grocery store, she bought a large can of ground black pepper.

As she drove to work, she slipped the baby baseball bat under the driver's seat, and slid the pepper right next to her seat, between it and the emergency brake.

Pepper in the eyes, she thought. No one can keep on going with pepper in their eyes.

Positive Oats was busy when she arrived at work, and Abbie couldn't find a close parking space. Okay, she thought. I'll move the car later.

Abbie was quickly drawn into her work, helping with the customer rush, closing down the salad bar, checking the shelves, and filling in wherever she was needed.

By the time the store was closed and cleaned, she was immersed in counting boxes and checking inventory sheets. She waved absently as the cleaning crew left, and turned back to the boxes, eagerly examining the new products, figuring out where to place them on the shelves.

She cleared off the weekly "specials" rack, returning the merchandise to its regular shelf space, and set up the new display. She double-checked the day order forms against the in-stock inventory, crossed off two items, and added one.

When she finished her work, she wrote down her hours, and then just wandered the aisles for a while. She breathed in the mixed odors of the shop—spices, spicy teas, the earthy vegetable scent—while she admired the display of new vitamins, minerals, and supplements. She found herself drawn repeatedly to the new liquid supplement for vegetarians.

I'm not exactly a vegetarian, Abbie thought. But I don't eat much meat. And it's such a neat, old-fashioned-looking bottle. . . .

Finally she gave in and took one of the heavy brown bottles to the counter. The cash register was shut down, of course, so she wrote out an employee's charge slip, wincing at the cost. Even with the employee's discount, eighteen dollars was a lot to pay for twenty-four ounces of something she wasn't positive she needed. She tucked the bottle into her backpack.

It wasn't until she put on her jacket and hefted her much-heavier pack that she realized she'd never moved the car. Remembering the car brought back the full weight of worries, and her idea about making herself an even more visible target, inviting attack.

She switched on the store's night lights and

the security system, and took a last deep breath of spice and earth as she slipped out the door, activating the automatic night-lock. The door swung shut with a solid thunk, locking itself behind her.

I love that store, she thought, trying not to look like she was carefully checking the parking lot for lurking shadowy figures . . . which she was definitely doing.

For five hours I was busy, happy, and safe, surrounded by health and healthy people. Now I'm back in the world of invisible enemies.

And I had the dumb idea to lure them out into the open? How crazy can I be?

She couldn't help hurrying a little across the lot, her heart thumping until she got the car unlocked and was safely relocked inside it. She brushed her hair back from her face, straightened her jacket, and propped her backpack on the passenger's seat.

She took a deep breath, then whistled it out in a "Phew!" Silly, she thought. I was scared out there in the dark. Like a little kid. And I'm fine. Nothing got me.

She put her seat belt on, started the Subaru, and backed out of the parking space, headlights on and radio playing. She put the car into "drive" and it sputtered. "No!" Abbie told the car. "This is not the time to have problems."

The engine smoothed out and Abbie sighed, half-gritting her teeth, afraid to trust it completely. But it took her neatly out of the lot, uncomplaining.

Okay, Abbie thought to the car. Just get me home, and I'll call Mom's mechanic in the morning. No more problems, okay?

But the car didn't answer, and it didn't respond, either. It accelerated sluggishly, and Abbie punched the radio off, listening to the car as it grumbled and hesitated.

Her heart contracted in instant panic. "I hate this!" she shouted, banging the steering wheel. "Cars are supposed to start, and go. That's all! None of this chug-chug stuff! Come on!"

She pushed the gas pedal harder and the car surged forward, though it sounded ragged, as if it were limping on three wheels.

It's not going to make it home, Abbie thought, her hands tensing on the wheel. She turned away from the highway, taking the back route, afraid of stalling in the high-speed traffic.

Mentally, she scanned her route. She'd never clocked the mileage, but it was a cross-country run, not a few-mile jog. I can do it, she thought. But I don't want to!

She rolled the window down to listen to the

engine. It sputtered, sounding too loud and uneven. The night air blew across her face, biting, sharp and cold.

"Come on, come on," Abbie urged the car. "Help me out, here. Get me home. I'll never ask another thing of you, just please, please get me home."

She'd never heard the engine sound so rough. No matter how hard she pushed on the gas, the car was struggling, slowing. She'd only made a mile or so from work.

No! Abbie thought, steering toward the side of the road.

The car groaned and sputtered to a halt.

Abbie shouted, "No!" but there was nothing she could do. She turned the key. The engine turned over raggedly, protesting, but did not catch.

Abbie hit the steering wheel again. "How can you just stop in the middle of the road?" she yelled.

The silence of the night closed in around her, and the breeze through the open window iced Abbie's hands, nipped in at the neck of her jacket.

I have to walk, Abbie thought. Or sit here. Those are my choices.

There must be a telephone between here and home. I can call a tow truck.

Abbie turned the key to "accessories" and rolled up the window. She grabbed her backpack and jumped out of the car, locking the door, holding the handle up as she slammed it. She stuck the keys in her backpack.

As her panic at the car's betrayal faded, Abbie's mind turned to practical matters. She was cold, and her pack was heavy.

And she was alone.

Alone and cold, on a dark and windy night in the middle of nowhere.

Abbie shuddered, looking around at the distant streetlights, the deep shadows, the disabled car.

I'm in trouble, she thought.

This is very bad.

My weapons! she thought. She scrambled to unlock the door, feeling around under the seat. Her fingers closed on carpet fuzz and dust, and a crumpled tissue.

No child-size baseball bat.

Abbie's hand scrabbled across the seat to the space between the seat and the seat belt.

Empty.

No pepper.

Her brain reeled. Someone's been in the car.

Did someone disable the engine?

She was suddenly certain. Her stepmother

kept it serviced, and it had never given anyone a second's trouble. Why would it suddenly quit now unless something had happened to it?

Someone did something, she thought grimly. She wished she had the slightest idea how cars ran and what to do when they quit running.

She straightened her shoulders, relocked the car. Okay, she thought. I wanted to flush him out . . . or her. This is my chance. If he's watching.

Of course he's watching.

Oh, Abbie, she thought. Don't be stupid. Get out of here!

# Chapter 25

Abbie grabbed her backpack and ran, but she knew there was no safe place to run to. There was a lot of dark, empty road between her and home, and nothing at home to assure her safety.

Her backpack swung on her shoulder, whacking her with every step. She knew there was a phone kiosk back at the little shopping center where she worked, and she almost headed back there until she remembered the OUT OF ORDER sign. It had been there so long, she'd gotten used to it.

She tried to think where the next closest telephone would be, but they all seemed so far away. There was entirely too much space and time between her and a phone.

All around her, boarded-up buildings and empty parking lots stood, ghosts from a more prosperous time. A few weed-riddled vacant fields, a couple of brave businesses, closed for the night . . . and a lot of dark.

Abbie trotted on, considering her options. The Subaru had not picked a very good area to quit on her, but it wasn't hopeless. The urban renewal program meant a lot of new businesses were going in around here. There had to be an all-night gas–grocery within a mile or so, or a hotel with a night clerk.

Hotel! Abbie thought. The credit card! I could stay in a hotel . . . or I can stick with my plan to stay in plain sight, do my normal things . . . go home, on foot, and be alert.

Abbie slowed her pace to a rapid walk, slipping the straps of her pack over her shoulders, wearing it instead of carrying it. Inside were her credit card, her purse, her identification, her keys — things too important to abandon, even if the pack was heavy.

Wait a minute! she thought, glancing back at the car. What am I doing running away from the car? If someone disabled it, they'll be looking for it. They'll come to the car to find me.

She turned around, headed back toward the Subaru, alert for a good hiding place. I'll hide and watch, she thought. That's the only way I'll find out who it is. Then I'll know. I can figure out what to do, once I know who I need to watch out for.

She heard a vehicle, heard the gentle noise of tires on asphalt, and before she could even think what that might mean, she found herself propelled by some primitive survival instinct, propelled into the recessed doorway of a boarded-up shop.

Dry leaves, blown by the wind, crunched beneath her feet and she froze, leaning into the shadows, watching.

A pickup truck crept by, its headlights off, its driver shrouded in the secrecy of night.

Joey! she thought. So it was Joey all along.

But Clif has a pickup, too. In fact, so do hundreds of people.

She eased herself forward, sliding her head out of the doorway just far enough to see, and watched the truck pull up to her car, watched someone shine a flashlight at it, then watched the truck swing around in the road and head back toward her.

She flattened herself in the shadows again, then gasped as the flashlight shone across her feet.

He's looking for me.

If he wanted to help me, he'd be calling my name.

The light flashed above her head. Abbie pressed herself into the corner, the pack digging into her back. She was barely breathing, her eyes closed.

She heard the truck roll on by.

Whose truck? she thought, trying to rebuild it in her mind, searching for some identifying detail. Joey's truck was older than Clif's, a darker blue. She hadn't paid any attention to the license plates on either truck . . . and with the headlights off, there was nothing to light the plates on this truck, anyway.

When she could no longer hear the truck, Abbie relaxed a little. I still don't know who, she thought, slumping. I lured them out into the open, and it didn't help at all. Now what am I going to do?

The wind picked up a little, scuttling leaves and papers, making a strange ticking-scraping noise at the edge of the doorway. Her shoulders tensed and she shivered in cold and fear, then almost laughed as a paper cup skittered by.

A few flakes of snow fell, slanted at her face by the wind, followed by more flakes. She shivered again. The wind whipped her jeans against her legs like the touch of icy hands.

I have great options, Abbie thought. I can stand here and freeeze, or I can go out there and be stalked by a phantom pickup truck.

As she thought the words, the truck returned.

He doesn't even have to stalk me, Abbie thought. I'm a sitting duck.

# Chapter 26

As Abbie watched, the truck pulled up next to her car. A figure got out of the truck, leaned back in, and then stood again, a grocery sack in its arms.

The figure was too far away, and too obscured by coat, hat, and snowflakes for Abbie to tell anything about it. She watched it unlock her car, open the door and lean in, watched it straighten again, rummage in the bags, and then fiddle around on the passenger side of the Subaru, near the rear bumper.

Then the person got back into the truck, and the parking lights flicked on. The truck made a sharp left turn and bumped up into a field, rapidly disappearing in the snow.

Abbie thought about how many times she'd left her keys — house and car on the same ring — in her jacket pocket hanging in the locker at school. She thought of George, opening lockers and then keeping quiet about it.

Anybody could have had copies made, she realized.

Abbie ran to her car. The gas tank! she thought, realizing what the fiddling around must have been. He poured something in the gas tank! So the car will explode if I try to start it again?

She backed away from the Subaru, and after a moment's hesitation, ran after the truck. I need to know who it is, she thought, following the tracks. Enough snow was sticking to the ground that the trail was just visible.

She followed it across the field and up an embankment. She trotted around a corner, and a huge shape loomed up.

Abbie skidded to a halt, recognizing the old sugar mill.

*Clif! His special place that only he knows about!*

She swallowed hard. Clif, she thought. I hope it isn't Clif!

She hurried on, drawn by the mystery, by the need to know who was tormenting her, by the need to end both the mystery and the torment.

She followed the tracks into the parking lot and slowed her pace, remembering the potholes and chunks of cement. The snow flattened everything, and she couldn't tell where it was safe to step. She could barely see the tire tracks now; the snow was filling them in, but she could make out enough to tell that they went straight, toward the river.

More shapes loomed up, and Abbie recognized trees. She remembered a little jogging path that ran parallel to the river and wondered if it was wide enough for the truck to drive on.

Then she heard a voice, carried in distorted waves, tossed about by the wind. She could only make out some of the words. ". . . can't trust you . . . keep hitting . . . her later . . ."

She flattened herself against a tree, listening. The wind blew damply from the river, and Abbie realized the sounds must have been coming from that direction.

She crept from tree to tree until she saw a gouge in the white snow, dirt showing. She paused to listen again, hearing no more voices, only grunts. In the swirling snow ahead of her she saw the truck between two trees, someone standing outside the open driver's side door.

Abbie scurried away from the path the truck had taken, circling to get a better view, a more protected view of whatever was going on.

As she drew slowly, quietly nearer, keeping

to the darkest shadows beneath the trees, she stopped suddenly, gasping in horror as the figure beside the truck closed the driver's door, reached in through the open window, and then stepped back.

The truck drove straight down the embankment and into the river, bobbing briefly, then sinking nose-first.

Abbie stood, frozen in shock.

The truck had not been empty.

There was somebody inside!

# Chapter 27

The figure turned and trotted back the way the truck had come, and Abbie's head pounded and her vision faded as she saw that the figure was wearing HER hat on its head, HER scarf wound around its face, HER sweatshirt.

Wasn't that the same sweatshirt Taylor had on the night we went to the movies?

The figure disappeared in the snow, and Abbie turned numbly back to the river.

At the sight of the truck's tailgate sticking up from the black water, Abbie leaped into action.

She shrugged off her backpack, unzipped her jacket and threw it aside, slipped out of her sneakers, and ran into the water, gasping at the cold. She grabbed for the tailgate and pulled herself along the side of the truck bed, sinking deeper into the cold water, fighting the tendency to float.

The water can't be too deep here, she thought. The truck didn't sink completely. I've got to get him out! Whoever it is. I've got to!

She took a deep breath and plunged her head under, feeling for the window frame, holding on, fumbling for the door handle. She finally wrestled the door open and felt inside, feeling loose fabric . . . but her lungs were aching, and she had to breathe.

She surfaced, gasping, knowing that the person inside had been submerged much longer than she had . . . was in much worse shape . . . lungs filling up with water as she filled hers with air.

Her legs were so cold . . . water weighted her down as it soaked into her clothes . . . wind and snow stinging her face . . . Abbie took another deep breath and pulled herself down again, knowing she had to drag the person out this time because she might not be able to dive again.

She felt in the truck, grasped the fabric — an arm? A jacket? She tightened her grip and pulled, but the body came too slowly, resisting. Abbie let go of the truck's frame and forced herself inside, grabbed onto the body with both hands, and pulled, her mind one roaring, black, swirling determination.

The legs! she told herself. Stuck under the steering wheel.

She reached down and grabbed what she hoped was a knee and yanked it sideways toward the door.

Her lungs were heaving, her body so cold it felt sluggish. She knew, then, that she was too late. While she'd been goggling at the running figure wearing her outer clothes, this person had drowned.

The body popped free and began rising toward the surface. Abbie was so startled she nearly lost her hold on it, but as it rose, so did she, breaking the surface with a harsh gasping indrawn sucking of pure fresh air, air that hurt her throat . . . that felt like pure joy.

She grabbed the truck bed with one hand and towed herself and the body along, handhold by handhold, till her feet touched the muddy slope, her legs buckling, then operating on their own, disassociated from her conscious command, crawling up, the body floating behind her.

She heard a feeble cough, and that small sign of life gave her access to some reserve of strength. Without knowing how, Abbie dragged the body to shore and straddled it from behind, pushing on its back in a vague hope that would help clear the lungs.

She rolled it over and noted in distant shock that it was Joey as she pinched his nose, tilted his head back, and blew into his mouth.

She could only hope she was doing things right. She'd seen mouth to mouth only on TV shows, and who knew how accurate they were?

But it was all she could think to do, and after what seemed like years, Joey coughed again, then suddenly rolled his head sideways and spewed out river water. She helped him sit up, and he coughed, gasping, choking, spewing water and vomiting.

But he was alive.

He was also dazed, trembling, shivering. He did not recognize Abbie, did not speak.

Blood oozed from his head and down his face.

Abbie fumbled with Joey's wet jacket and shirt, her fingers almost numb, awkward on the clammy fabric.

She finally got them off, grabbed her own dry sweatshirt-jacket, and bundled Joey in it. She folded his wet T-shirt into a bandanna shape and tied it snugly around his head, trying to stop the worst of the bleeding.

The wind had died down, for which Abbie was grateful; she was practically an ice cube in her wet clothes. But the snow was falling harder, in huge, fat flakes.

Already there was a thick coating on the ground.

We can't sit here, Abbie thought dully. We would truly freeze to death. And Joey needs a doctor. I need dry clothing. And blankets. And hot tea.

She got to her feet. Joey just sat, looking blank. His breathing was shallow, and his entire body was shaking with shock and cold.

Abbie reached down and took his hand. "Come on, Joey. Get up." She tugged, and finally he lurched to his feet.

"Let's go find someplace warm." She draped one of his arms around her shoulder, wrapped one of hers around his waist, sliding it beneath the jacket. Then she saw her snow-covered backpack, lying where it had landed when she stripped it off.

Leave it, her brain told her.

But my purse, my credit card . . . She bent down and snagged it up, wriggling into it one strap at a time. It might be a little bit of a windbreak, she thought. Better than nothing. She wore it in front in order to least disturb her hold on Joey.

She found it did act as a slight barrier between her and the snow, though its added weight was almost too much as Joey lurched along beside her, leaning too heavily sometimes so that she staggered.

She wondered how far they would make it before they collapsed completely. Whenever she hesitated, Joey tried to sit down, so Abbie trudged on, aiming — she hoped — toward the mill's parking lot and the nearest street that would take them somewhere . . . any place there might be a phone, or warmth, or a car to flag down.

Slowly they went forward. Abbie's teeth were chattering so hard, she was afraid she was chewing her tongue to shreds. Her hair must have frozen into icicles for it scraped against her cheeks like icy spikes, and she literally ached all over from the cold.

They stumbled through the potholes and over cement chunks and at last out into a street, and Abbie couldn't believe her luck as headlights appeared a minute later.

She waved her free arm frantically, and the car drove toward them, slowly at first, then picking up speed.

At last! Abbie thought, starting to sag in relief.

The car bore steadily down on them, faster and faster.

Abbie whirled and threw herself sideways,

Joey tumbling along as a dead weight, collapsing onto her, crushing her onto the sidewalk.

She wasn't even surprised as her brain belatedly registered the fact that the car that had almost run them down was her own disabled Subaru.

And she knew, as well as she knew anything in her half-frozen state, that the Subaru was turning around, would come back and try again.

# Chapter 28

Beside her, Abbie could hear Joey wheezing, making little noises of pain.

"Get up," Abbie said, flapping his arm. "We've got to run."

Joey did not resist her pull, but he couldn't seem to help her efforts, couldn't seem to grasp what she wanted.

He's getting worse, she thought, pulling harder. What if he's bleeding inside his brain? He'll die right in front of me.

She could hear the car returning as she got Joey to his feet, and she drew his arm across her shoulder, grabbed the jeans fabric at his waistline, and lurched off in a frantic, futile attempt to outrun the car.

The tunnel! she thought. The tunnel of bushes! I could hide him in there and run for help. He'd be sheltered, at least a little, and nobody would find him . . . except Clif! He knows about the tunnel.

But she had no other ideas and almost no more strength. She knew it was hopeless, but she staggered on anyway.

This time the car missed them by inches, and Abbie landed on Joey. She heard his breath whoosh out, heard him cry out in pain, and knew they would never make the comparative safety of the tunnel.

Abbie started shaking.

It's over, she thought. Joey can't run anymore. Even if I could hide him somewhere, I couldn't run for help. I'm half-dead and three-quarters frozen, and besides, anybody could follow my tracks in the snow.

Her pack was pressing against her chest, and Abbie slipped it off. She could hear the Subaru returning for the third pass at them, its engine racing.

She grabbed Joey under the arms and dragged him backward, back away from the road, then left him in a heap. She grabbed her pack and ran back toward the road, thinking vaguely that the car couldn't hit them both at once.

The Subaru almost sang as it came toward her. The pack was so heavy . . .

So heavy . . .

Almost in a dream . . . definitely in a nightmare . . . Abbie reached inside the backpack, grabbed the heavy bottle of nutritional supplement, and threw it directly into the windshield of the oncoming car.

# Chapter 29

The windshield exploded, the car veered, then spun out of control. It hit the curb on the right side of the road, the high-speed impact flipping the right side of the car up. It flew sideways through the air, then toppled to the ground, landing driver's side first, skidding along the pavement in a shower of sparks and noise, finally coming to rest on its side, mangled.

Abbie screamed.

She ran to the car, screaming, screaming, running, slipping in the snow. She had to check, had to see if the person was still alive. Every instinct told her to run the other way, to get away, to get help for Joey and leave the maniac in her stepmother's car to fend for itself.

She couldn't.

She simply couldn't run away without doing something.

She knelt by the wreckage, then lay down on the ground to peer in the window . . . at the unconscious, bleeding, but still breathing driver.

"Brett!" she said, and her throat hurt.

"Brett! Oh, no!" Abbie lay on the ground in the snow and glass, with gravel poking at her, and wept.

"So now you know," Brett said, his voice weak, but clear.

"But why, Brett? Why, why, why?" Abbie asked.

"My dad . . . walked out on me." Brett's voice was barely more than a whisper. "Mom was all I had left. Everything was okay until I had to share her with you. I've wanted you out of my life since the day I met you."

"But you taught me to swim!" Abbie knew it sounded stupid, but she didn't care. She still couldn't believe what she was hearing.

"I threw you in. I hoped you would drown."

"You showed me how to catch a baseball!"

"I was hoping . . . " Brett coughed. "To knock your head off with one fast pitch when no one was looking."

"No." But Abbie felt the truth of his hatred. "What did you do to the car?"

"Water in the gas tank. Two cans of Heet

evaporates it out again. No one would have known."

"Why Joey?"

"Someone had to be guilty. Joey set himself up for it, being obsessed with you already." He coughed again, his eyes closing.

"It almost worked," said Brett. "With you gone, I would have been okay."

"No," Abbie said sadly. "I don't think you'll ever be okay."

# Chapter 30

Abbie lay back against the soft pillow of the bed in her own bedroom. It felt good to be home. It felt good to be safe.

She turned over to look at the clock, and that's when she heard it — a soft tap-tap-tapping at the window.

Not again, she thought. When will this nightmare end?

Slowly she got to her feet.

There was someone there. She could just see his face through the glass. She walked across the room, and then . . .

The window exploded, and Abbie screamed.

"Calm down, Abbie," her father's voice said. "It's over. All over. You're okay."

Abbie shook her head, to clear it. She was still in bed, but not at home. She looked around the darkened hospital room, finally locating a clock. "How long have I been here?" she asked. "Is it really noon? I've got to get ready for work!"

"Today's Sunday. No work for you."

"Sunday!" Then the memory of all that had happened came back to her.

"Brett?" she asked.

Her father shook his head, his face gray and old-looking, drained. "His mother is with him. She's so sorry, Abbie. She feels so bad for you."

"Is he going to live?"

"He had a concussion, and there's some concern about brain injury. A lot of cuts and bruises. The air bag saved his life. Oh, Abbie. I'm so sorry, too. We didn't know Brett was sick. We didn't even know he was jealous. He always seemed so good with you.

"We got back from our little cruise," her father continued. "And found Brett's message at our hotel. We couldn't make sense of it, so we called. We spent several hours calling and never got an answer. We finally got smart and took the next plane home. The house . . . no one home, locks on the bathroom door, an odd message on the answering machine . . . and that thing on your bed. We called the police."

"They filled you in."

Her father nodded. "And we called Taylor. She thought you should have been home from work already, so we called the police back and convinced them to search for you. I guess Taylor called some guy named Clif?"

Abbie smiled.

"So they went out looking, and so did I. Mom stayed by the phone at home."

"Who found us?" Abbie asked.

"You don't remember?"

Abbie shook her head, and it made her dizzy. She raised a hand and rubbed her forehead. "Why am I here? I want to go . . . " She didn't finish the sentence because she realized it wasn't true. She didn't want to go home.

"The police found you first," her father said. "Then Taylor and then Clif and I, about the same time. And you're in the hospital because you have a raging case of pneumonia, not to mention a close call with hypothermia, and numerous cuts and scrapes." He covered her hands with his, swallowed hard. "You had a busy night. Abbie? I want you to know . . . I promise you, Brett will never bother you again. He'll be in hospitals or jails for the rest of his life."

"And Joey?"

"He's singing your praises to everyone who comes near him. You saved his life several times over. I think you have a fan for life."

Abbie groaned.

She didn't remember dozing off, but when she opened her eyes her father was gone, replaced by Taylor, holding flowers.

"From Clif," she said. "He couldn't stay long."

"Taylor . . . " Abbie reached for a tissue and wiped her cheeks. "I owe you an apology. I suspected you. I'm so sorry."

"Shhh!" Taylor said. "It's okay. I wasn't there for you when you needed me. I was acting weird."

"I should have known you had a reason," Abbie said.

"How could you know if I didn't tell you? You can't read my mind."

"I still should have known," Abbie insisted.

"Well, I'm not going to argue with someone in a hospital bed. How about we just agree to forgive each other and do better next time?"

"Deal," Abbie agreed. "Except there better not be a next time! I have one other thing to say to you, Taylor, and then for the rest of our lives, this will be a closed subject. Got it?"

Taylor nodded.

"I threw a bottle of nutritional food supplement for vegetarians at the car," Abbie said. "And it stopped him."

"I know," Taylor said. "It's not like I was

in love with him, Abbie, and even if I had been, I wouldn't be now, knowing what he did to you and Joey, and what he was trying to do. Nobody will ever blame you."

"You missed the point."

"So fill me in."

"The point," Abbie said, "is that health food saved my life."

Taylor looked startled. Then she grinned. She held her hand up solemnly. "I promise," she said, "that I, Taylor, will never try to make you eat a french fry again."

Abbie grinned sleepily. Taylor is right, she thought. I am a fanatic. I may have to work on that . . . later.

There was a knock on the door, and a hospital aide pushed it open. "Visitor," she announced, pushing in a wheelchair containing a heavily bandaged but broadly grinning Joey.

"Tell us what happened!" Taylor demanded.

"Why were you with Brett?" Abbie asked.

"First you showed up at school all bruised and cut," Joey said. "That scared me, so I started following you. And then I started getting phone calls saying you were going to get hurt."

Abbie nodded. She remembered telling Brett about Joey following her to the movies, being obsessed.

"Were you at Mocha's?" Abbie asked.

Joey nodded. "I saw you meet those guys, so I knew you were safe. I figured you'd be a couple of hours, so I left. And when I got back, you were gone."

He flushed. "I couldn't let something happen. Not if I could help it."

"So you broke my window, watching over me?"

"I didn't. I never went to your house. Well, I drove by a lot. That one time all the lights were on all night and I tried to call."

"That was you!"

"I was afraid something was wrong. So I went back and watched and I saw you outside. I figured you were guarding the house."

Abbie nodded.

"And Friday, you went out with Clif and I watched. I didn't know if he was the one or not." He flushed again. "Then you went to Taylor's house and then to work. I knew you'd be fine there, and I was going to follow you home, anyway, so when I got the last call saying you wouldn't get home alive . . ."

"You went to the store and found Brett there," Abbie guessed.

"Yeah. He said his car had been messed with and he thought yours might have been, too, and we had to find you. He said, 'Look at this!'

and I got out to look, and wham. Next thing I know I'm in the truck and Brett has this little tiny baseball bat and wham again. I wake up here."

Abbie yawned. She realized quite a few things had changed . . . and one of them was how she felt about Joey. Somewhere in the darkness of the river they'd forged a bond, and it had solidified during the rest of that nightmare night. I'll never love him like a boyfriend, she thought. But a brother . . . ? I'm missing one of those.

"See? Was I right or what?" Joey asked. "Abbie, you are some kind of fabulous!"

"You're sick," Abbie muttered.

"Am not."

"Am, too." Abbie felt her eyelids drifting shut, and she let peace wash over her.

# POINT CRIME

*If you like Point Horror, you'll love Point Crime!*

## Specials

For Point Horror afficinados everywhere, three deluxe
hardback editions from your favourite
Point Horror authors...

**1: The R.L. Stine Special**
*The Baby-sitter I, The Baby-sitter II, The Baby-sitter III*

**2: The Diane Hoh Special**
*The Fever, Funhouse, The Invitation*

**3: The Caroline B. Cooney Special**
*Freeze Tag, The Stranger, Twins*

# *Point Horror*

# COLLECTIONS

Are you hooked on horror? Are you prepared to be scared?
Then read on for three helpings of horror...

*Point Horror*

Dare you read

# NIGHTMARE HALL

*Where college is a*
*scream!*

**High on a hill overlooking Salem University hidden in shadows and shrouded in mystery, sits Nightingale Hall.**

**Nightmare Hall, the students call it. Because that's where the terror began...**

Don't miss these spine-tingling thrillers: